CHESTER HOUSE WINS THROUGH

Irene Smith

THE CHILDREN'S PRESS
LONDON AND GLASGOW

First printed 1967

Christine Lane.
9.2.68.

CONTENTS

CHAPTER ONE

A NEW TERM

"OUR NEW head girl evidently means business," Rita bemoaned.

"A good thing, too," Shirley, a pleasant faced senior, answered, "if it improves the kids' behaviour. They were little demons all last year."

"You can't expect them to behave like sixth formers at their age," Joyce answered easily.

"I thought Helen made a fine speech," Pauline, another house-prefect, said. "Pointed, too; especially about the bad feeling between the Houses," she added ruefully.

Rita bristled. "That's not our fault," she returned. "We don't *ask* to be treated as inferiors just because we're day girls."

"Not all the boarders treat us like that," Shirley objected peaceably. "Only a few."

"With Brenda giving a lead to them," Pauline added pointedly. "Now she's head of Merton we shall know what to expect from *that* House."

"Brenda wouldn't deliberately influence her House against us, I'm sure," Shirley answered fairly.

"But she's always making nasty cracks at our House," Rita growled.

"I don't understand," Ruth, a new prefect, joined in, rather bewildered by these sudden revelations from her seniors. She was still in the Upper Fifth herself. "Why should they treat us like outcasts? We haven't done anything!"

"That's just it," came in quiet tones from the head of the table. "We *haven't* done anything."

Five heads turned in stunned silence towards the head of the table where Alison their new House captain sat silently doodling on her note-book. She lifted her head and looked levelly round on them all. "That's just it," she repeated deliberately. "We *haven't* done anything."

They stared dumbly at her for a few moments. All but Shirley, whose eyes were twinkling. She and Alison had been close friends during the whole of their school years. Knowing Alison so well, and her plans for the future, she was prepared for the abrupt interruption.

Rita found her voice first. "What do you mean?" she demanded.

"Exactly what I said," Alison returned. "For the last year we've drifted along, doing nothing at all to improve our status amongst the school Houses—until now," she finished with emphasis. "We've reached so slack a state that nobody can respect us."

Even Joyce was startled out of her usual lethargy by the last remark.

Alison went on. "I know it's an awful thing to say about one's own House. I'm as keen on it as you are. But we *must* face facts. Our House at present is the weakest link in the school."

"I don't see that," Rita objected truculently.

"No?" Alison lifted her eyebrows. "Whose Juniors and Middles caused the most trouble during the last year?" She paused. "*Ours*," she said, when nobody spoke. "Ours, with fifty per cent. more reports than any other House. I've looked it up in the reports book, and that's enough proof."

"That's probably because the school pres. had a down on our House," Rita muttered, unwilling to admit that even she was shaken by the news.

"That's not fair," Shirley protested. "Our youngsters *were* far worse than the rest. Some of them . . ." She hesitated.

Alison's mouth twitched. "Some of them," she finished for her, "especially my twin sisters, were absolutely appalling." Her voice sobered. "I agree with what Shirley was too polite to say," she said. "My young sisters were in more than their share of mischief and something must be done about it."

Shirley chuckled. "They're a jolly pair," she said. "Jane gets round all of us with her wiles at times."

" Then she mustn't," Jane's sister said firmly. " Nor must the other scamps in the Middle and Junior schools. They must toe the line if we're going to pull our House up. I've been thinking things out; there's a lot to be done. If you'll back me up we'll *make* the rest of the school appreciate us as a House. On our merits, too. If we put our heads together we can do it, I'm sure."

There was silence; everyone looked thoughtful. It was Joyce who broke the spell.

" Two pep talks in a few hours," she moaned with affected weariness. " First Helen, and now Alison. It's enough to drive any poor prefect into leaving school and going out to work for a rest."

They laughed, Alison joining in.

" Yes," Pauline complained. " I was looking forward to a good hard year's study. My hopes of a scholarship are fading already."

" Nonsense," Shirley replied bluntly. " Most prefects have exams to face, but that's no excuse for letting things slide. Alison's too loyal to mention it, but that's why the House is in its present state. Our last head was too wrapped up in her books to see what was happening."

" She meant well, though," Alison said quietly. " She did well for the school in the scholastic line, so we mustn't condemn her."

" But apparently it's our job to clear up the mess which she left," Pauline remarked dryly. " Discipline and games down to zero."

Rita roused herself. " You needn't worry about games," she retorted. " That's my department. I mean to win a few matches this year if I have to wring the necks of the little wretches to make them play."

Alison's face brightened. " Good for you, Rita," she said. " That's the spirit. We'll make the rest of the Houses look to their laurels. I've one or two ideas of my own, too, which might help. Are there any other suggestions before we discuss them?"

There was a short pause. Then Joyce spoke.

"Yes," she said slowly. "Though what I say is more a protest than a suggestion. Our House is not what it should be, I'll admit, but we've been working under a handicap, and that is the lack of a room of our own. Why should we have to discipline our girls with a lot of gaping infants from other Houses looking on? Their prefects can attend to that sort of thing in their own studies."

"Hear, hear!" grunted Rita. "And why should we have to wait after school until the school prefects have gone before we can borrow their room for our meetings? Some of us have buses and trains to catch. It's most inconvenient!"

Alison and Shirley looked at one another. Alison gave a little laugh. "It's strange," she said, "but that's a matter I was about to bring up. Shirley and I have been poking around in the school these last two or three days with the same grievance in mind." Her serious face lit up, and her eyes twinkled. "In the tower is a room which is not used, except for housing a few boxes and other rubbish. Phillips, the caretaker, says it isn't used because it's up too many stairs, and away from the rest of the school."

"Do you think the Head will let us have it?" came in an excited chorus from the rest.

"I don't know, I haven't asked her yet," Alison admitted. "I thought I'd wait and see what you all said first. We could offer to clean it up ourselves, if you're not all allergic to spiders. Why not finish our meeting another time, and pop up and have a look at it now? That is, if you busy people are not in too much of a hurry," she added with a humorous look at Rita.

They all rose to their feet laughing.

"Lead on, Macduff," Pauline ordered dramatically.

CHAPTER TWO

THE TWINS

"Gym twice a week," Gillian complained with a little sniff. "I can't help it if my legs shoot the wrong way every time. Miss Preston needn't shout at me about it, I don't *want* them to. There must be something wrong with them."

Jane eyed the offending legs critically. "They *look* all right," she said. "Just a bit skinny, that's all. Perhaps you don't eat enough," she suggested.

"If either of us eats much more, Mummy'll have a fit," Gillian declared. "She says it's like feeding a couple of ravenous wolves now."

Jane nodded. "I expect she's right," she said. "I never seem to fill myself up, and you don't do too badly. Can't understand why you don't get fatter. Your legs might go right then."

The fair, bobbed-haired twins sat side by side in the old woodshed, which, to save nervous strain on the rest of the family, their father had given them for their use and the housing of their small menagerie. A pair of rabbits wriggled their noses in the hutches above them, and a puppy and tortoiseshell cat played happily together in the corner. In the window hung Joey their parrot, who, with erratic coaching, had built up quite a collection of remarks and comments which he was apt to bring out at awkward moments.

"Do you think," Gillian suggested hopefully, "I might catch something before next Tuesday, so that I needn't go to gym?"

"No," Jane answered crushingly. "We had enough of that last year. You kept catching things and we missed no end of fun. That's why your legs are so stiff, I suppose." She took one of Gillian's feet and waggled her leg up and down in a professional manner. "It's your joints, I expect," she diagnosed. "We must do something about it."

9

Gillian looked more cheerful. She had faith in Jane's ideas despite dismal results from them in the past. "How?" she asked.

"We'll ask Daddy," Jane decided.

Mr. Carstairs suppressed a sigh when he saw his twelve year old daughters approaching him—most people who knew them did. He was not at his best just then. He was struggling with a fault in his car and, not being of mechanical turn of mind, his temper was not improved by it. The bonnet cover was up, and he was prodding hopefully at various spots in the engine when Jane sidled up to him.

Jane peered with interest into the open bonnet. "It has internals something like ours, hasn't it?" she remarked chattily, with vague memories of a recent biology lesson. "What's wrong?" she demanded tactlessly.

Her father took a deep breath. "If I knew that, I shouldn't be wasting my free afternoon looking for it," he answered, exasperated. "Anyway," he demanded suspiciously, pushing back his hair with oily fingers, "what do you two want? If it's more pocket-money, you can't have it."

Jane eyed him reprovingly. "Really, Daddy!" she protested in hurt tones. "You must think we've got mer-mer-mercery minds." She meant mercenary. "Anyway," she added with dignity, "we couldn't be asking for *more* pocket-money, because we haven't had any this week. You kept it for that window which got itself broken. We still have sevenpence-ha'penny between us, so we shouldn't be *asking* you for money, should we?"

Mr. Carstairs put his hand in his pocket resignedly. "Here," he said, passing over some coins. "For goodness' sake take it and go away and play, or something."

Jane took the money and giving her twin half, tucked the rest in the pocket of her shorts. "Thanks, Daddy," she said. "We didn't come for that, but it'd be rude to refuse a present. We wanted to ask you what is the best thing for stiff joints?"

Mr. Carstairs looked up from fingering the greasy car engine. "Stiff joints," he answered. "Why oil, of course."

Jane looked dubious. " Oil?" she inquired. " What sort of oil? Olive oil or castor oil?"

Mr. Carstairs smiled. " No, lubricating oil," he answered amusedly, wondering what was in the minds of the twins. He supposed it was something to do with the doors of their rabbit hutches, and he believed in encouraging independence. " It depends on the size of the joints, whether they are large or small."

Jane eyed Gillian's knees speculatively. " Fairly large," she said.

Mr. Carstairs wiped his hands on an oily rag. " I'll get you something," he said, and went to look in the garage.

" Here you are," holding out a bottle and brush. " I can't spare the oil-can. You'd better brush it into the joints instead."

" *Brush* it?" Jane demurred. " Won't it tickle?"

" Tickle?" Mr. Carstairs looked bewildered. The twins were too much for him at times. " Rub it in well, then," he said, anxious to get rid of them and on with his task. " If you can't manage it, I'll come and see to it later," he offered. " You can keep the oil," he called after them, as, to his relief, they retreated towards the woodshed.

Shortly afterwards, the twins sat in the woodshed, brooding over the bottle of oil as it stood on the bench before them.

" It looks awfully messy," Gillian said.

Jane picked up the bottle and tipped a little oil on her finger. " Mm, it does a bit," she agreed. " But we'd better start," and picking up the bottle she tipped a generous portion of it on to Gillian's knees, and began to rub them vigorously.

Gillian's knees began to take on the hue of ripe tomatoes. " You're doing it too hard," she complained.

Jane paused and looked at her reproachfully. " Daddy said rub it in *well*," she told her. " You want to be able to do gym, don't you?" she demanded. " And stop Miss Preston shouting at you?"

Gillian nodded. " But you're hurting," she protested. " And —and it *smells*."

Jane sniffed. " It does a bit," she agreed. She sat on her heels and regarded her twin thoughtfully. "Everybody'll know what we're up to if you go about reeking like that," she said. She pondered on the matter for a few moments. "I know," she continued, firmly corking the bottle. "We'll rub you at bedtime. Not just your knees, but all over your joints. We can wrap something round you so's you don't make your sheets and pyjamas messy. You can get up early and have a bath before you dress, nobody'll smell you then."

Gillian was not very elated at the prospect. "A bath *early every morning*," she repeated, aghast. "I couldn't do it. We're never up in time."

"We *shall* be," declared her stronger-minded twin. "We'll borrow Mummy's alarm-clock. She'll be glad to lend us it if she thinks we'll be in time for breakfast for a change."

Gillian still looked dubious.

Joey moved restlessly on his perch. He thought he had been neglected for too long.

"*Jump to it!*" he ordered stridently.

Gillian sniffed. "It looks as though I shall *have* to," she answered him gloomily.

CHAPTER THREE

RITA MAKES A MOVE

THE GAMES COMMITTEE had been in private council. Their business was completed and they sat chatting together before dispersing.

"Hardly worth the fag of playing for the cup, is it?" Brenda remarked with mock resignation. "Your House'll romp home with it as usual, I suppose."

There was a laugh in which Helen, the head of the school, joined in.

"Defeatism run riot," she commented in her low, pleasant voice. "It's about time someone *did* wrench that cup from

Russell House," she added teasingly to Jean. "How many years has your House won it? The last five years?"

"Four," Jean corrected modestly.

Brenda grunted. "All the same you'll be receiving a challenge from Merton in the near future, so keep a date for us."

A comical look crept over Jean's face. She was head of Russell House, as well as games captain.

"Thanks," she answered with a twinkle. She paused. "That's the second challenge we've had to-day," she then revealed.

"Oh," Brenda answered idly. "Who's the other from?"

There was slight hesitation. "Day girls," Jean quietly answered.

Brenda sat up straight. "What!" she almost shouted. "Really! Of all the colossal cheek! They haven't even a proper team. They couldn't challenge *anyone* last year. And then to pick on the crack House team. Nerve I call it, and I hope you told them so, Jean."

"Actually, I've decided to accept the challenge," she replied, and saw the approval in Helen's eyes. "To be honest, I felt a bit like Brenda at first. I have so few free dates, I intended to keep them for a stiffer fight for the team. There'll be some grumbles from them about it."

"Don't blame them," Brenda muttered. "I still think it's cheek on the part of the day girls."

"I don't think it was meant to be," Jean answered seriously. "Actually," she owned, turning to Helen, "it was the remarks in your speech the other day about bad feeling between the Houses which decided me. I thought it would be a small gesture towards improving things. When I spoke to Rita about it, I felt I'd done right. She's very keen," Jean went on. "She obviously intends to stir things up in that House. She said she chose our team to challenge, because with only a scratch team at present she thinks it would be better for them to meet opponents they needn't mind losing against. I thought I'd fix a date for later on to give her a chance to pull her team together."

"Good for you," Helen said. "A little encouragement won't hurt them. With Rita coping with games, and Alison as head, we can expect a few changes in that House this year."

" Then I hope they'll turn their attention to disciplining their juniors, especially Alison's twin sisters," Brenda commented pointedly. " Nobody knows what those two will be up to next. Had a tussle with them this morning, but I'm not sure who won."

" Oh?" Jean asked, interested. " What were they up to this time?"

" Goodness knows," Brenda answered in disgruntled tones. " Caught them tearing up and down the tower stairs. At least," she amended, " Gillian was doing all the tearing up and down, carrying something or other each time, while Jane directed operations from the bottom and timed her at it."

" I suppose they gave some explanation?" Helen suggested.

" Explanation?" Brenda answered. " I expect it was supposed to be one. Couldn't make it out. Jane talks one into a stupor at times. She told me some long rigmarole about their having permission to be there, and that Gillian had to do all the running up and down to exercise her legs. She suggested that there was something wrong with them. I didn't know there was, did you?" she inquired of Helen.

Helen laughed. " Not to my knowledge," she said. " Though I dare say they had permission to be in the tower. Some of the day girls were clearing out their new prefects' room. Alison asked the Head if they could have the old lumber-room in the tower for their own."

" Why?" Brenda demanded.

Helen put down the pencil she was holding and spoke seriously. " For a reason which even the Head admits that she had overlooked. None of us realised that that House had no room of its own where it could privately thrash out its problems. We have our studies where we can attend to that sort of thing."

" I hadn't thought of it," Jean owned.

" The room was in a terrible state," Helen went on. " The day girls were working on it on Saturday, and already it looks a different place. From what you say, Brenda, I gather that the twins were helping. Though why it should be necessary for Gillian to have all the exercise, and Jane give the orders is as much a mystery to me as it is to you." And she gave a low chuckle. The twins amused her vastly at times.

"Alison has certainly lost no time in getting things going," Jean said. "Term's only been started a few days, and she and Rita have already wakened things up."

"Yes," Helen agreed. "Knowing Alison I should say it's the start of a wider campaign, too. We boarders will have to look to our laurels," she teased as she rose to return to her study.

CHAPTER FOUR

DAY GIRLS PLAN THEIR CAMPAIGN

"THAT'S next week's duties settled," Alison observed with satisfaction. "Now we can get down to the business we had to leave last week."

"If the rest of the suggestions turn out as well as the one which gained us this room, we shan't grumble," Pauline remarked with a contented glance around.

Alison felt none too confident as she scanned the agenda before her. She lifted her head and looked round on her fellow prefects. "I'm afraid some of the items here will not be quite as acceptable as that one," she told them with a smile. "But I hope you'll consider them carefully before you blow up about them." She paused. "We'll start with a suggestion which I believe none of you will find too objectionable. It's about our name as a House. We've always been referred to as ' Day Girls' House ', which personally I think rather weak. I don't see why we shouldn't have a proper name like the other Houses. Do you?"

They agreed.

"Then can any of you suggest a name?" Alison asked.

They lapsed into thought. Every now and again someone came out with a proposal which was received with groans or shakes of the head from her fellow prefects. At last Joyce made a suggestion which was agreeable to them all.

"As this is Millchester College, and most of us live in Millchester, why not call it Chester House for short?" she proposed.

"Do you think the Head will agree?" Pauline asked.

Alison put down her pen. "I hope so," she answered. "You'll realise that all of these suggestions are subject to her approval. They will first be put before the school council. Not that I should let disapproval from the council stand in our way," she added firmly, "if the Head agrees."

Rita brightened. "You mean you'd ignore the council's comments, even Brenda's remarks?" she asked with interest.

"I do," Alison replied definitely.

"Good," Rita answered with satisfaction. "I'm sorry I can't be there to hear the fireworks. What's the next suggestion?" she added hopefully.

"Badges," Alison revealed. "Someone proposes that instead of just wearing the plain school hatband we should have a special house badge of our own like the other Houses."

"The girls in my Form would like that," Ruth said shyly. She had not yet reached the stage where she felt happy in voicing her opinions in front of her seniors.

"Well, I don't see that there can be much objection to it if the girls are willing to buy the badges," Alison answered her. "What do you all think?"

"As far as I'm concerned, it'll be the parents who do the buying," Pauline said dryly. "I'm always stony broke. But I dare say they'll bear the strain. I'm for it, anyway."

"Same here," Joyce agreed. "Though my objection is having to sew the wretched badges on," she added plaintively. "Nothing I stitch ever goes straight."

They laughed. Joyce was not famed for her needlework.

"Then it seems that except for those two mild objections that proposal is passed, too," Alison said when they were quiet again. She glanced at the agenda and hesitated. "The next item, I fear, may not be so acceptable," she remarked. "It's a proposal that we should abide by the same rules as boarders with regard to lock-up hours in the evening, which means that

no day girl should be out after that time without permission."
And she looked rather anxiously around at her companions.

There was utter consternation on the faces before her.

"But that's ridiculous!" Rita burst out. "We couldn't go anywhere, not to the cinema or anything."

"Not in term-time except with special permission," Alison calmly returned. "But neither can the boarders."

"But we're *not* boarders!" Rita returned furiously. "It'd be treating us iike a lot of babes."

"There's some point in it, though," Pauline observed slowly.

"Where?" Rita demanded truculently.

"We—ell," Pauline answered unwillingly. "After all, we're all supposed to be studying for exams. There isn't much time to go rampaging round to places."

Rita was affronted. "*Rampaging!*" she retorted indignantly. "I don't *rampage* when I occasionally go out in the evening instead of stewing over fusty books all the while."

Alison smiled briefly at them both. "I expected a few fireworks over this," she said. "It's a big thing, I know, but let's talk it over as calmly as we can. I've brought the matter up, partly because of remarks which some of us have overheard from the staff and seniors of other Houses. Some of our older girls seriously abuse the privilege of being free to go out in the evenings. That's not meant as a hint for you, Rita," she added carefully. "Some girls go to places of which the Head doesn't approve."

"But why should we all be restricted because of a few who play the idiot?" Rita demanded.

"They can't be controlled if there's no rule against it," Shirley pointed out.

"That's the difficulty," Alison agreed. She paused. "It's like this. I've heard unofficially that, because some of the girls are abusing the freedom we have in the evenings, the Head is thinking of making restrictions to prevent the school from getting a bad name. If she does, it would be more of a slur on our House than if we tackled the matter ourselves. There's no other way of dealing with it."

"No, I don't think there is," Joyce agreed thoughtfully.

" So you're in this ridiculous proposal, too, are you?" Rita retorted with slight sarcasm. " It seems that the whole thing was more or less arranged beforehand."

Joyce looked taken aback; she was never one for an argument, anyway.

Alison came to her support. " That remark was most unfair, Rita," she said with quiet authority. " Joyce had no knowledge of the proposal until now and she has a right to voice her opinion."

Joyce gave a little smile at Rita which softened the rebuke.

" Rita has got me wrong," she said. " I'll admit that the suggestion is a bit of a blow to me, too. If it's passed, I shall miss the orchestral concerts I indulge in occasionally." Joyce was a keen violinist.

Pauline found her voice again. " Yes, and there are some literary lectures coming off which I'm keen on hearing," she owned.

" But one would be able to get special permission for that sort of thing," Shirley observed. " Joyce's music and your lectures are part of your education. The boarders are sometimes allowed to go to things of that sort."

Alison consulted her watch. " Shall we leave the matter for a few days as you feel so strongly about it?" she suggested. " I know I've rushed you about it, but I was anxious to get some offer of ours in before the Head makes a move. It'll mean sacrifices from all of us if we make the offer, but I think the Head would appreciate it."

" *And* the other Houses," Shirley said.

" What's it got to do with them?" Rita demanded.

" We—ell," Shirley hesitated, searching for a tactful way of expressing her thoughts. Rita was so fiery it was best to tread warily.

It was the shy Ruth who spoke. " They—they resent our having privileges which they haven't," she ventured. " At least, some of the boarders in my form do, when our girls talk about dances and things they've been to."

" Exactly," said Alison. " But I think we'd better leave the matter for the present, and go on to the next item. We'll tackle the subject again when we've thought it over."

" I shan't alter my opinion," Rita declared stubbornly.

" No?" Alison smiled at her. " Remember we're only anxious to do what's best for our House," she reminded her. " Anyway," she went on in more business-like tones, " the next item should calm us down a little. It is suggested——"

She got no further. Quick footsteps were heard. There was an angry thud on the door which then shot open, and Brenda, the head of Merton House, stood in the doorway, glaring round at the assembled prefects. " Exactly what I expected," she said in cutting tones. " Gossiping here while the rest of your House raises bedlam in the school."

There was a stunned silence. Alison's voice when she spoke was more controlled than her feelings. " Perhaps you'll come in and shut the door if you've a complaint to make," she suggested. " This is supposed to be a private meeting."

Brenda flushed further in her annoyance. She pushed the door to with her foot.

" I came to ask you to do your duty by your House," she replied stiffly. " If you prefer not to be disturbed I can easily refer the matter to Helen."

It was more than Rita's fiery nature could stand. Brenda always got her on the raw, anyway. She jumped to her feet. " Of all the cheek . . ." she exclaimed angrily.

" That will do," Alison interrupted quietly. " Leave it to me, please. What seems to be the trouble, Brenda?"

" How do you explain that practically the whole of your juniors were making a dreadful din careering round the hockey field with no one in charge?" Brenda demanded fiercely. " They should all have been away home ages ago."

Alison rose to her feet. " I'll go and look into it," she said.

Brenda stayed in her position in front of the door. " There's no need to," she answered. " I sent most of them home for you to deal with to-morrow. The ringleaders are waiting downstairs. One of them has been most impertinent, and I won't be spoken to in that manner."

" Who are they?" Alison asked.

" Your twin sisters," Brenda answered forcibly. " As you might know."

Alison suppressed a sigh.

Brenda noticed it and her voice softened. " As usual they have some rambling excuse for being where they shouldn't be at this hour," she complained. " I gather that it was supposed to be with Rita's approval." And she looked very straight at that prefect.

" *My* approval?" Rita exclaimed in startled tones.

" So I understood," Brenda returned. " From what Jane said I gathered that you had *asked* them to do it, which appears a little odd to me when you weren't there to supervise them."

Shock had taken the fire out of Rita. She looked completely bewildered. " But I couldn't be. I know nothing of it," she blurted out.

Brenda seemed half-convinced. " Possibly," she agreed. " When Jane makes explanations matters are apt to get a little confused. But I won't have impertinence from her," she said firmly to Alison. " I'll leave you to deal with it."

" I'll have them up now," Alison quietly said.

" Not while I'm here," Brenda answered, moving towards the door. " I have my own House to see to, and I've been delayed enough already." She turned as she opened the door. " That's one advantage we have over you," she said pointedly. " We do know *where* our Middles and Juniors are out of school hours. *And* our seniors. It would be a lot easier for everyone if your House had a little less freedom." With this parting shot she turned and closed the door behind her.

Alison's mouth was set but she made no other sign of having heard the last remark. " Ruth, fetch those two up here, will you, please?" she said.

Ruth obeyed. Rita looked over at Alison in the silence which fell. " I *didn't* know anything about it," she muttered.

" No, I'm sure of that," Alison agreed.

The twins' eyes flickered with concern when they entered the room and saw the assembled prefects—they were unprepared for that. But Jane soon recovered herself.

" We ought not to be long. It's getting awfully late, and it'll be tea-time," she observed with an accusing look at her sister. " Mummy'll wonder where we are."

"Naturally," Alison returned drily. "You should have thought of that before."

"We did," said Jane. "We'd have been gone by now if it hadn't been for Brenda butting in," she complained. "We meant to be home in time for tea."

"I'm sure you did," Alison agreed patiently. "You never willingly miss a meal. What we want to know is why you are still here after five o'clock?"

"We—ll . . ." Jane began to prevaricate. "You see, Brenda kept us quite a bit, and then we had to wait downstairs while you talked to her, and——"

Alison's voice cut in in steely tones. "That will do," she said. "We've no time for your usual rigmarole. Get to the point. What were you doing on the playing field after school hours?"

Jane looked hurt. "Why, playing hockey, of course," she said. "Practising *hard* when Brenda stopped us. Weren't we, Gill?"

"Yes," Gillian agreed obediently. "Practising *hard*." She did not look quite as confident as her twin. She always left the talking to Jane, anyway.

"Then did you have permission to be on the field—from Jean or someone?" Alison suggested.

Jane's brow puckered in thought. "Er—not exactly," she owned. "But Rita did tell us to do hard practising. And we had to do it somewhere, didn't we?"

Rita groaned. "So *that's* where I come into it, is it?" she complained. "I did tell them to practise as much as they could," she admitted. "But I meant at home, or somewhere like that—not on the first eleven field."

"But we *can't* practise at home," Jane protested. "Daddy said none of the neighbours are safe. You know he did, Alison. Three windows got broken last week. We just can't *afford* it. We're saving up for something else important, aren't we, Gill?"

Gillian nodded in solemn agreement.

"The field was being wasted," Jane continued in reproving tones. "You shouldn't waste things."

"*Waste* things?" Alison repeated. Though she had lived with the twins for years she did not always find it easy to follow their line of thought.

"Yes, *wasted*," Jane persisted. "Nobody on it," she added kindly, in case her point had not yet reached the simple minds of her elders. "We didn't notice it until we were out of the school gates, and going by the hedge round it. Did we, Gill? Then when we looked through it, the hedge I mean, we saw that there wasn't anybody on the field. It's wicked to waste a field with nobody on it, when there's lots of girls like us who want to play so's we can practise, and beat all the other Houses like Rita said. And . . ."

Rita sighed again in the interval while Jane paused for breath. Alison grasped the opportunity to check her sister's flow.

"But didn't it occur to you to ask about it before you used it?" she asked.

Jane was nothing if not honest. "Well, yes, I suppose it did," she confessed. "But they might have had to say 'no'. We didn't think there'd be anyone to ask, anyway."

"You mean by that, I suppose, that you waited until you thought we'd all gone home," Alison said coldly. The quick look the twins gave her confirmed her guess. "But you were mistaken. Brenda was still in the school and so were we. Which brings me to another point. Brenda complained that you were rude to her. Is that so?"

Jane fidgeted uncomfortably. "Only me, not Gill," she said. "She didn't say anything. Only that awful Bren—— I mean," she hastily substituted, "Brenda said it was just what she expected from day girls," she indignantly revealed. "She said we were the worst juniors in the school. And—and then I said——" she hesitated.

"Well?" Alison prompted.

"Well, I——" Jane did not sound quite as sure of herself. "I said that we weren't, and that we'd rather be day girls than belong to her beastly House, 'cause they were a lot of snobs. And——" She faltered again as she caught her sister's expression. "And—and I said she wouldn't stop us practising, 'cause we were going to practise and practise till we beat her beastly House, and then she wouldn't call us names."

There was a dead silence. Alison pulled herself together.

"You were very impertinent," she said quietly. "You will apologise to Brenda to-morrow."

Jane looked startled. "But that means saying I'm sorry, and I'm *not* sorry," she protested. "It'd be telling a lie."

"You *will* apologise," Alison repeated. "You *should* be sorry, because you've let your House down instead of helping it." She paused to let that sink in. Apparently it did, judging from the shocked look in the twins' eyes. "I'll deal with the rest to-morrow," Alison went on. "You two, as ringleaders, will lose all your break and recreation times for the rest of the week." She turned to Rita. "I'm sorry, but that means that they are out of games for the time, too. It'll be poetic justice perhaps," and the corners of her mouth twitched.

The door closed behind the hungry and dispirited twins. An eloquent silence fell on the seniors.

Then Rita sat up straight. "When did you say the next school council meeting is to be held?"

"I don't think I mentioned the time, but actually it's to-morrow at five o'clock," Alison replied.

"So that's why you were trying to rush the suggestions through?" Rita commented.

"Well—yes," Alison agreed. "If we had been in agreement on them I should have tried then to get them before the council. Otherwise it means waiting for another fortnight."

There was a little pause. "I think we all *do* agree," Rita then said unexpectedly.

They stared at her.

"Yes," she said. "After that little interlude with Brenda I've changed my mind. I'm not having her going around making cracks at us like that. We'll meet her on her own level, even if I don't get to the cinema for a while," she grinned.

"*Good*," said Alison, smiling back at her. "Actually as prefects I don't expect we shall be too hemmed in."

"Do you think you can put it before to-morrow's meeting?" Pauline asked anxiously.

"I'll have a good try," Alison promised. "I'm afraid if we

wait another fortnight the Head might get her proposition in first."

"I've another suggestion to add to the list," Rita interrupted, a comical twist to her mouth. "That is, if the rest agree."

"Oh?" said Alison in surprise.

"Yes," Rita continued. "I propose that instead of our w—wasting the field after school hours," here her voice shook with laughter, "I should ask permission to give extra coaching occasionally to the kids who are keen."

They all agreed to that. "A jolly good idea," somebody said.

"But not *this* week for the twins," Alison reminded Rita with a twinkle. "Even if they *are* responsible for the idea they mustn't get swollen heads."

They laughed again.

CHAPTER FIVE

ALISON'S UNFORTUNATE DAY

THE NEXT DAY it seemed to Alison as though everything and everybody conspired against her. Actually it was not so—the real cause of her misfortunes was a sleepless night of pain which put her out of tune with everything.

She was thorough and conscientious in all that she undertook and that was why she had been appointed as head of the day girls. The Principal knew that the House was badly in need of a keen and strong-minded leader.

Alison's mind was still full of plans for the betterment of her House when she lay down to sleep. But she could not rest. As soon as she became drowsy a nagging pain started in her face and jaw which caused her to lie dozing and tossing until daybreak.

The most sensible thing to do, she thought as she dressed in the morning, was to stay indoors and get advice about the pain. But her mother must not know, Alison decided. There was so much to see to at school, she could not afford to stay away on that particular day. If she lost the chance of putting her suggestions before the school council that evening, her prefects would feel that she had let them down.

She arrived down to breakfast feeling exhausted and depressed.

From the opposite side of the table, the twins, with thoughts of their restricted freedom in mind, watched her with reproachful stares as she plodded painfully through her food. Eventually with a glance at her watch she excused herself and hurried off to prepare for school. It was later than she thought; the school prefects arrived early at the school to supervise the younger girls in the cloak-rooms. Alison realised that she had no time to spare. As she wheeled her bicycle from the shed, she noticed that she had two flat tyres. It was strange, she thought, as she stooped to examine them; they had been in good order the previous evening. Then she found that the screws were off both valves.

A reprisal of the twins, she decided vexedly, as she reached for her pump. But there was no pump there. Alison was a tidy soul; she knew that she had left it in its proper place. Feeling completely frustrated, Alison considered for a moment. Her sisters had already started for school in an unusual urge to be early for once. She would be late for duty now, anyway, Alison decided. Would it be quicker to hunt round on a possible fruitless search for the pump, or to walk to school which would take her a good twenty minutes? She decided to walk. Her aching face seemed to be in league with the twins for it gave a few extra malicious stabs to add to her troubles.

Prayers were just over when she reached the school. She reported to Helen straightaway.

"Well, accidents happen to everyone," Helen said with a smile. "There's no need to be so agitated about it."

"Well, it wasn't——" Alison began, and then hesitated. There was no need to drag her sisters into it. They were in everyone's bad books as it was.

"I'm sorry I missed my cloak-room duty," she said instead. "I hope everything was all right."

" Well——" Helen answered her honestly. " There was a bit of a ruction with some of the Third Formers. Excitement about something which happened yesterday afternoon, I understand. But Brenda dealt with it."

Alison swallowed. " So she told you about it?" she said resentfully.

" Yes," Helen's voice was kind. " She couldn't very well help it; as you weren't here we thought you were ill. But you can deal with it yourself now."

Another bit of bad luck, Alison thought exasperatedly. She would have preferred to make her own report on the previous evening's incident. And of course it would have to be Brenda who had to deal with the indignation meeting of the Third Formers. No doubt that was one reason for the twins' urge to be early for school. She had the other culprits to interview some time that morning. She must see them at break-time, she decided.

But she did not. When the break bell rang she received a summons from the Principal. Miss Frazer only wished to re-arrange the timetable for her studies, but it left Alison no time to deal with the previous day's culprits until after morning school. When they had gone it was time for her lunch. With no bicycle she had to walk home, hurriedly.

She arrived home for the meal, still in pain, and also in a very disgruntled mood. She had had no time to prepare for the after-noon meeting, or to interview the twins about her bicycle. When she entered the dining-room they were already at the table—pictures of innocence. They were less talkative than usual, which was not a good sign with the twins. Jane fidgeted as she stared impatiently at her elder sister plodding painfully through her first portion.

Then Jane gave an enormous sigh to draw attention to her-self. " Do you think, Mummy," she asked sweetly, " that Gill and I might be excused? We ought to be out in the garden; we haven't had any fresh air this morning. We shan't get any this afternoon either," she added pathetically. " And there's not much time before school."

"No fresh air?" Mrs. Carstairs exclaimed, falling for the bait. "That's ridiculous. Why?"

Jane lowered her eyes. "Some stuffy person in the school stopped it. I think we should be out of doors while we have the chance. May we go?"

They departed hurriedly as their mother gave her consent.

Mrs. Carstairs looked disturbed. "Really, I don't know what the school is thinking of, keeping girls of that age indoors all the while," she worriedly complained. "It can't be good for them, especially for Gillian. The doctor says she needs fresh air. I think I'll mention to Miss Frazer that she shouldn't be kept indoors too much."

Alison cleared her plate and looked up.

"I shouldn't, Mother," she said quietly. "She has nothing to do with it, and it would only make more trouble. *I'm* the stuffy person who's keeping them indoors."

Her father chuckled.

Mrs. Carstairs looked affronted. "Well really!" she exclaimed. "The things you girls take upon yourselves. It's ridiculous. You should know that Gillian——"

Mr. Carstairs had been watching his elder daughter.

"Gillian's all right," he broke in with quiet authority. "She looks better now than she has for a long while. Anyway," he said with a twinkle, "if Alison can control the twins by keeping them either indoors *or* out, she has my approval."

Alison smiled back at him. There was a bond of understanding between them. "Thanks, Daddy," she said uncertainly, "I think I needed that." She pulled herself together. "If you'll excuse me," she added quickly, pushing back her chair. "I must get back to school; and I want to catch the twins first, if I can." She paused on her way to the door. "We have a meeting at five," she said. "So I shall have time only to dash home before going back to school. Don't worry about tea for me, Mother; I can make a cup if I want it."

Mrs. Carstairs looked at her husband. "These young people," she complained.

Her husband rose from the table. "I'm thinking it's our

eldest daughter who looks more in need of special care than Gillian," he said thoughtfully.

Alison was wily. Years of living with the twins had made her so. She left the house by the front entrance instead of the garden door which she usually used, and crept quietly around the house, concealing herself as far as possible behind the bushes as she neared the back garden. She was just in time to see a whisk of short navy skirt as its owner disappeared round the side of the woodshed. She made a quick dive, and grabbed Jane by the back of her collar as she attempted a hurried departure. She gave her a sharp shake.

" I've got you now," she said grimly. " So you can stop wriggling. " *Where is that pump*?"

Jane opened her eyes wide. " Pump?" she inquired with suspicious innocence.

Alison gave her another little shake. " Yes, I said *pump*," she answered impatiently. " It's no use trying that injured innocence trick on me, I've no time for it." She looked at her watch. " I'm going upstairs to get ready for school," she said. " If those tyres are not fully blown up, and the pump in its proper place when I come down in five minutes Helen will hear of it."

Jane's mouth dropped open. " Helen!" she gasped. " But you *can't*. It's nothing to do with school."

" It *is*," Alison sternly retorted. " You made me late for duty and prayers this morning, and Helen had to hear of it, though *without* names. However, she'll get them if I have to walk this afternoon, and am late again for duty."

Jane sniffed as she wriggled free. She had no wish to have dealings with Helen. " I think it's jolly mean of you," she said.

Alison's face gave a vicious stab. " I believe I'm capable of *any* sort of meanness to-day," she said savagely as she hurried away.

The twins must have worked hard. When she came back five minutes later both bicycle tyres were firm, and the pump hung neatly in its place. The twins had vanished. Alison breathed a sigh of relief.

The afternoon passed with lessons, and a series of further

interruptions which left Alison not a single moment free in which to prepare for the evening's meeting. By the time four o'clock came and the school was dismissed she was almost ready to weep with frustration and pain. Even then there were two or three members of her House who waited behind to see her.

Somehow she *must* find a few quiet moments in which to sort out her ideas before the meeting, she thought desperately as she cycled rapidly towards her home. She entered the house by the garden door and hurried quietly up to her room, where she locked herself in and took out her notes.

By then it was half past four. In the quietness of her room she worked rapidly, sorting out her ideas and trying to work out a method of approach which would make the new proposals acceptable to the council. Though she did not intend to be deterred by their opinion, she felt that it would be a help to have their goodwill and blessing on the efforts of her House.

It had gone ten to five, she found to her consternation, when she finished her notes. Still, she thought as she hurriedly put her papers together, she could just reach the school in time if she rushed.

It was not to be. As she moved rapidly downstairs the dining-room door opened and her mother appeared. She looked considerably annoyed.

"Really, I have the most inconsiderate children," she exclaimed. "Here am I with your tea ready especially for you ever since four o'clock, and you hide yourself away upstairs without telling me. You're old enough to have more thought. You'd better get it now. It's still on the table."

"Thanks, Mother, but I can't stop for it now," Alison rushed towards the door. "The meeting's at five."

"Nonsense!" her mother was firm. "It's raining, and you must have some food before you go out. I know what those meetings of yours are. You'll come home dripping wet after seven o'clock with no food at all inside you. It's asking for trouble."

"But I can't *wait*," Alison protested agitatedly. "I'll have something to eat later." She did not want to hurt her mother's feelings. It had meant an effort on her part to have the meal

B

ready for her so much earlier. Mrs. Carstairs had taken to heart her husband's remarks on Alison's wan appearance.

"You will have it *now*," she said. "You're only wasting time arguing. You should have come down for something to eat before now, instead of staying up in your room."

"I *can't*. I've already been late once to-day," Alison still protested. "And—and it's an important meeting. I *must* be there," she added, by now on the verge of tears.

"I don't know why you were late," her mother firmly returned. "But you're having something to eat before you leave this house. You've scarcely eaten anything to-day. I'm not as blind as you think I am. So come along, and no more nonsense."

Alison had to obey. She struggled to fight back the angry tears as she tried to swallow some of the tempting meal her mother had prepared. She was so upset that every mouthful was like sawdust.

Alison had inherited her stubbornness from her mother. It was not the first time that their wills had clashed. Mother was so *dense* on some matters, Alison furiously told herself.

It had gone twenty past five before Alison had eaten enough to satisfy her mother.

She left the dining-room hastily, and hesitated as she reached the staircase again. Should she stay away from the meeting altogether? There was not much point in going now. She could easily plead sickness, for what with the pain and the upsets of the day she was feeling far from well. Her head ached abominably. But no, she decided, to stay away would be cowardice on her part. She had promised her prefects she would do her best, and she must do so, whether there was any possibility of putting anything before the council or not.

She grew angrier than ever as she cycled through the rain. She had prepared for the meeting with such high hopes only half an hour before, but now she had lost heart altogether.

CHAPTER SIX

HELEN STEPS IN

IT HAD gone half past five when Alison reached the school. She still seethed with indignation and disappointment as she pushed open the door of the prefects' room, and slumped angrily into her seat.

Helen was speaking, but on Alison's abrupt entrance a silence fell. There was a short, awkward pause while apparently everyone waited for the expected apology. But none came. Alison was too full up with her emotions to speak. Instead she glared angrily around as though daring anyone to protest. A look of relief had appeared on Shirley's face on her friend's arrival, but now a puzzled expression took its place.

Helen glanced at Alison's face and said nothing. She consulted her notes as though there had been no interruption.

"I was speaking about your duties," she calmly began again in her pleasing voice. "Some of you have been forgetting that you must not exchange them with another prefect without permission; it leads to difficulties when you do. I expect that really I was not supposed to see it," she continued humorously, "but I've noticed quite a bit of juggling with duties this last week."

One or two new prefects looked guilty.

"I try to arrange the duties as conveniently as I can," the head girl went on. "If any of them are at difficult times for you let me know when I give them out, if you can. If not, ask me about changing them before you do so, please."

Jean as second in command felt in a position to speak. "Of course, skipper," she pointed out, "there are times when it's difficult to keep closely to that rule. In an emergency when a pre. has gone sick or something, and you aren't available, one might have to step into the breach and take over someone else's duty."

Brenda grunted. " They certainly *might*," she said feelingly.

Since her stormy arrival Alison had sat with her head lowered, staring down at the table almost as though she was in a trance. She felt dazed with pain. But at the last remark she sat up straight.

" Meaning *me*, I suppose?" she said curtly, staring angrily at Brenda.

Brenda looked surprised, for she had spoken thoughtlessly.

" I *hadn't* meant it so," she answered coldly. " If you refer to this morning's affair I didn't take over your duty intentionally. I went into the junior cloak-room to speak to one of my House and found turmoil amongst your juniors. Naturally I had to stop it as there was no other prefect there."

" *And* report it to Helen instead of to me?" Alison persisted. It was unlike her to be quarrelsome, but something seemed to be egging her on; possibly it was the necessity of relieving herself of some of her pent-up feelings.

Shirley moved uneasily. Really! What had got into her friend? She was absolutely throwing away her chances of bringing anything before the meeting with hope of success.

" Naturally I reported it," Brenda answered.

" *And* last night's affair which was my business, too?" Alison demanded, her resentment getting the better of her.

Brenda flushed with annoyance, and was about to make an angry retort when Helen banged on the table.

" If you two have personal differences, please keep them for another time," she said firmly.

Brenda swallowed. " Sorry, skipper," she said. " I had no intention of making an upset."

" Neither have I," said Alison. " But I resent the continual digs Brenda makes at our House."

Brenda took that in. She had been seething ever since Alison's tardy arrival. " Yet even I," she said slowly, " never come to a meeting over half an hour late without apologising, and with the one intention of disturbing everyone there."

Helen glanced at Alison's stricken face, and spoke quickly. " I asked you both to drop the matter," she said sternly. " We'll have no more of it, please. We'll go on to the next business," she went on in quieter tones. " Jean has something to say about games."

They quickly dealt with the remaining business. Brenda recovered herself, though she was quieter, and said very little. Alison made no further comment, except to give churlish assent or dissent to each motion.

At length Helen pushed aside her notes. " Has anyone any other business before we close the meeting?" she asked.

There was silence. Shirley glanced anxiously at Alison. But Alison sat with her mouth firmly shut, staring down at the table before her.

" Right," said Helen, and they pushed back their chairs.

Alison was edging from the room when Helen tapped her on the shoulder. " Can you spare me a minute before you go?" she asked in low tones. " I must speak to one of the others first, but I won't be long. Wait in the next room if you like."

Alison escaped from the unwelcome companionship of her fellow prefects, and slipped along the corridor to the small room which the head prefect used during school hours.

Shirley watched her go, and her heart sank. It meant further trouble for her friend from Helen, she supposed. Being the faithful friend she was, patiently Shirley stationed herself outside the school door to await her friend and escort her home.

Alison looked around the little room as she waited. It was the most peaceful spot she had found that troubled day. It was restful for her aching head. She was in for a reproof from Helen, she supposed, as she sank thankfully into one of the chairs, but it did not seem to matter now. She had let her prefects down after all their high hopes, that was what troubled her. None of the council would have wanted to listen to her that night. *How* her wretched head and face ached. She hoped that Helen would not be long. All she wanted was to get home and crawl into bed.

Helen came in, and Alison braced herself for the onslaught.

Helen's voice was friendly. " Sorry to keep you," she said. " You look done in. It's chilly, I'll switch the fire on for a few moments. Come nearer and get a heat," she suggested.

The quiet considerate words were almost too much for Alison. She stared at Helen and swallowed quickly.

"I'm sorry about to-night," she apologised huskily. "I couldn't help being late. I ought to have apologised before, I know, but I——" She faltered.

"Felt too full up?" Helen suggested.

Alison nodded and tried to speak.

Helen looked at her. "What is it, Alison?" she asked gently. "Something's wrong, you're not yourself at all to-day. Can I help? That's what I'm here for."

Alison could stand no more. She lowered her head and burst into tears.

Helen crossed over to the bookcase where she stood silently gazing at the volumes for a few moments.

When she turned back, Alison was mopping disgustedly at her eyes.

"I'm sorry," Alison faltered.

Helen smiled. "No need to be. You'll probably feel better for it."

Alison gave a final rub and a wintry smile. "I don't know what made me so idiotic. I suppose it's this wretched face-ache. It's been giving me beans all day."

Helen looked concerned. "You mean you've been in pain all day!" she exclaimed. "Why on earth haven't you done something about it? You should have stayed at home."

"I didn't feel I ought to," Alison confessed. "I—I'd promised to do something to-day," she faltered. "B-but I didn't manage it. It's been an *awful* day," she finished shakily. "I've messed things up all round."

"Could you tell me about it?" Helen asked. "In confidence, I mean. It might help."

Alison told her everything except the details of the suggestions she was to have put forward that night.

"That was the last straw," she confessed wearily. "Mother keeping me back, and making me late for the meeting. I was in a furious temper by the time I arrived here, what with one thing and another. It was hopeless then for me to bring up any business at the meeting."

" Was it very urgent?" Helen asked.

Alison nodded. She gulped as she thought of her prefects' disappointment, and Shirley's reproachful eyes. " These are the notes of it," she thrust the papers forward. " But they're not much use now; it's too late."

Helen studied the notes while Alison watched her anxiously. Helen's face was expressionless as she read the items through carefully.

When she looked up, there was an odd look in her eyes.

" Do you mean," she said carefully, " that your prefects have agreed to these? To all of them, I mean?"

Alison nodded. " Yes," she said.

" I mean," Helen pressed, " particularly the one about lock-up time?"

" Well—yes," Alison replied, looking at her in surprise. Helen's manner was a little strange. " They didn't agree at first, but it was unanimous in the end."

" Well," said Helen sincerely, " I must congratulate you. How you managed to persuade them to make a sacrifice like that, I'll never know. It's more than I could have done."

" I didn't," Alison admitted honestly. " Most of them agreed reluctantly. But Ri—er one of them was dead against it at first, and it had to be unanimous to work properly. Actually it was Brenda who did the trick." And Alison gave a rueful little laugh, and told her of the happenings of the previous evening.

" Ah," Helen said when she finished. " If you knew Brenda as well as I do, you'd realise there's really no malice in her remarks. It's purely tactlessness. I must have a word with her about it. But we're straying from the point," she continued in more business-like tones. She gestured towards Alison's list of suggestions. " Did you especially want the council to see those?" she asked.

" I thought I had to," Alison answered uncertainly.

" Certainly not," Helen replied. " It's your House business, and nothing to do with the others. Why not take it straight to the Head?"

Alison's face lit up with hope. " Could I?" she asked.

" Of course," Helen answered. " Actually, I'd rather you did.

Apart from the delay before another meeting, I don't see why you should lay yourself open to criticism from the rest of the council. It's no concern of theirs. They couldn't have stopped you taking it to the Head, anyway."

" They certainly *wouldn't* have done," Alison said bluntly.

Helen laughed. " Well, there you are, you see. Take them to the Head and I'll back you up," she promised. She paused. " Now we'll get down to the business I kept you back for," she added with a teasing smile. " It wasn't to natter at you, as you seemed to expect. I don't think I dare have done that with you looking as fierce as you did. I wanted your advice."

" M-my *advice*?" Alison faltered in surprise.

" Yes," Helen replied. " The Head says we may have an extra senior on the council. The prefects have too much to do now that the school is growing so quickly. As you know, we have two representatives from each House at present. As you have more than double the number of girls in your House, we think the extra one should come from there. The decision will come from the Head, that is, officially, of course," she added with a twinkle. " But I'm not sure who to suggest. Shirley is on the council already, so it will have to be one of your other senior prefects. Who do you suggest?"

Alison considered the matter. " I don't really know," she said. " I don't think Pauline would be anxious to spare more time from her books. Joyce is reliable, but——"

" A little slow," Helen finished for her with a smile. " And Rita?"

Alison hesitated. " She's very efficient," she said slowly.

" But not very easy to handle, I gather?"

" No," Alison agreed. " But she has ideas, and she's very energetic. The trouble is that she and Brenda don't see eye to eye, and they'd probably clash."

" They would have to try not to do that," Helen said. " Anyway, think it over, will you, and let me know what you've decided to-morrow." She glanced at her watch. " Goodness," she exclaimed, " it's seven o'clock. We'd better be off."

They found Shirley still waiting patiently in the doorway, where she was sheltering from the cold and rain. She was relieved to see the two seniors approaching, apparently on the best of terms. There was a brighter look on her friend's face, she noticed.

"Good," said Helen, when she saw Shirley waiting. "Alison can do with an escort, she's not feeling too skittish. I shall have to hurry," she added, as at the gate she turned in the opposite direction from them. "It's lock-up time," she laughed teasingly. "To be a boarder can be a *terrible* handicap at times," she observed with mock resignation as she walked rapidly away.

Alison chuckled.

Shirley stared after the departing head girl. "What *have* you two been up to? My curiosity won't stand much more strain."

Alison's voice was warm with satisfaction. "We've taken the first step towards creating a new Chester House, I hope," she chuckled.

CHAPTER SEVEN

THE TWINS STEP INTO THE BREACH

"ALISON not down yet?" Mr. Carstairs remarked as he accepted his first cup of tea the next morning.

"No, she won't be for a day or two," his wife replied. "I've told her to stay in bed."

"Isn't she well?" Mr. Carstairs asked anxiously.

"She isn't," his wife replied. "She has a nasty chill, and I'm not surprised. She admits that she felt ill yesterday— neuralgia, and so on, and she went out last evening in the pouring rain. I should have put my foot down and stopped her, but she seemed so set on going to that meeting of hers. She wanted to struggle to school this morning, too, but I think she's feeling too ill to argue with me about it. There's no sense in it," she continued, "tramping about in the wet, and not allowing herself

...ie for a decent meal. It's asking for trouble—bronchitis or pneumonia, or something. She'll be lucky if she escapes them as it is. She——" She broke off at a sudden choking sound from where her twin daughters sat.

Jane's eyes were wide and her face red as, with difficulty, she gulped down a mouthful of cereal.

"Really, you two," their mother exclaimed in vexation, turning her attention in their direction. "Just look at your hands. I don't believe you've touched them since you cleaned out the animals' shed this morning."

"But they're *clean* animals," Jane answered reproachfully. "They haven't anything catching. And—and, anyway, we've had a *bath* this morning," she added desperately. "We shall catch cold, too, if we keep getting ourselves damp, like you said just now. And——"

"*Go and wash your hands*," Mrs. Carstairs broke in decidedly, to end the argument which she knew might otherwise go on indefinitely.

The twins gave up the struggle and hastily obeyed. Time was running short before school. They stared concernedly at each other before scrambling for the washbasin.

Gillian sniffed. "It—it was beastly of us to make her walk to school," she said.

Jane rubbed her nose with a soapy hand. Her conscience was troubling her, too. "We didn't *know* she was feeling bad," she ventured, "or we wouldn't have done it. It was decent of her not to tell Mother about us. We'll have to put it right somehow."

"But *how*?" Gillian inquired anxiously, her eyes filling. She must think we're *awful*. And—and," she added fearfully, her imagination running away with her, "if she's going to be ill with bron-bronk—bronkiosis or something like Mummy said, she might even *die*, and then we'd be *murderesses*."

Even Jane looked a little startled at this tragic picture. "But Mummy didn't *say* she might die," she protested weakly. "We mustn't let her. Anyway," she added after due thought as she hastily dabbed her wet hands on a towel. "We shall have to show her we're sorry somehow. We haven't any money left to buy her flowers like you should for ill people. Suppose," she suggested " we let her have our ration of chocolate for this week?"

" But it's only one bar between us now that we have to buy the oil," Gillian protested. " That isn't much. Couldn't we— couldn't we stop the oil and rubbing for a week, and buy something nice for her?"

" No," Jane answered decidedly. " You must keep on with it until you can do gym properly. It's working already, 'cause you said Miss Preston smiled at you yesterday instead of shouting at you. Anyway, you won't be so—so smelly now. The man in the chemist said we're using the wrong oil. He gave me some different stuff. He kept laughing," she added indignantly. " I can't see what there is funny about it. Anyhow," she went on more briskly, " we'll give Alison our chocolate this week. It'll show her we're sorry. And we'll be kind to her—really *kind*. It's bound to make her feel better."

Meanwhile, their parents had been having a private chat.

" I can't make those two out," Mrs. Carstairs remarked when the twins made their retreat.

" Why, dear?" her husband replied. " What have they been up to now?"

" Nothing. At least, I don't *think* they've done anything," Mrs. Carstairs answered uncertainly. " But it's so strange. They get up every morning now before I call them. Borrowed the alarm-clock, so that I shouldn't be worried, they said."

" Well, that's all to the good, surely," her husband sighed in relief. " I recollect that we've almost had to drag them out of bed before."

" But it's so *unnatural* for them," his wife protested. " It's such a job to make them clean themselves in the ordinary way. Now they insist on bathing first thing in the morning. Said they preferred it to the evening because it's more *healthy*."

Mr. Carstairs laughed. " That sounds like Jane."

" What they're doing with their pocket-money, I can't imagine," Mrs. Carstairs went on worriedly. " They spend every penny of it the first day they get it. When I scolded them about wasting it all on sweets and things, they said they didn't and that they allowed themselves only one bar of chocolate between them each week. It's most odd."

Her husband smiled. "Well, I dare say the mystery will be solved in time," he answered easily, as the door received a bang which heralded the return of his younger daughters.

He watched them from behind his newspaper as they took their seats. They looked rather subdued, he noticed, and there were traces of tears around Gillian's eyes. Maybe they had been quarrelling, he decided.

Jane disposed of her cereal, and then cleared her throat. "Do people *often* die of bronkiatosis?" she suddenly demanded.

Her father lowered his paper and stared at her. "Die of *what*?" he asked, in excusable bewilderment.

"*Bronkiatosis*," Jane firmly repeated. "What you get when you catch cold," she added patiently for his benefit.

"I—I think Jane means *bronchitis*," Mrs. Carstairs said helpfully in rather wobbly tones.

"Yes, that's it—what I said *bronkiatosis*," Jane answered earnestly. "Do people *die* of it?"

Mrs. Carstairs pulled herself together. "Occasionally," she answered, blinking the tears of mirth from her eyes. She helped herself to a piece of toast, and then suddenly paused as she was about to take the first mouthful. "Oh, my goodness!" she exclaimed, turning to her husband. "I'd forgotten the Simpson's luncheon party. That's to-day, but I can't possibly go with Alison in bed. I'd reckoned on her seeing to the lunch as it's Mrs. Tompkins' day off."

Her husband looked concerned. "It's rather important, dear," he reminded her mildly. "It won't do to upset the Simpsons if we can help it. We should be away for less than a couple of hours. Isn't there anyone who could relieve you?"

Mrs. Carstairs looked worried. "I know I ought to go," she said slowly, "but I can't think of anybody——"

"There's *us*," Jane said, offended. "We can look after Alison and cook the lunch for you if you tell us what to cook. We're nearly in our *teens* now," she added impressively. "We'd like to, wouldn't we, Gill?"

Gill nodded, though she looked a little doubtful.

"We do cookery in Guides," Jane continued to press. "We ought to have more practice. We do First Aid, and invalid cookery too. We can nurse Alison for you as well."

Mr. Carstairs laughed. "That's where I *should* draw the line," he protested. "We don't want her having a relapse. But why not let them have a shot at getting a meal for themselves?" he appealed to his wife. "They won't come to any harm, and they'd be here if Alison wanted anything."

"She won't want any food except a milky drink, and I could leave that ready," Mrs. Carstairs agreed. "But I don't like going with Alison so unwell. She mustn't get out of bed, and I don't think the twins——"

"We'd be awfully good," Jane interrupted, noticing signs of weakening on her mother's part. "We'd *promise* to be, wouldn't we, Gill?"

Their mother hesitated. "We—ell," she answered uneasily. "But you must hurry straight home from school. You leave at twelve to-day. I'll wait until you come, and I'll leave everything prepared. But Alison's not to be worried, mind. You can ring us up at the Simpsons' if there's anything wrong. Oh! that reminds me," she went on, "Alison has a note for you two to take to school, so you'd better hurry up. It's for the head girl, she says, and she wants her to have it as soon as possible before school."

The twins looked startled. "F-for *Helen*," Jane gasped. There were one or two little matters which, they were hoping, might escape the head girl's memory if they could manage to avoid her for long enough. "Helen's awf'lly important. Couldn't we take it to Miss Frazer instead if it's about Alison not going to school? Or Shirley?" she added hopefully. "She could give it to Helen."

Their mother eyed them suspiciously.

"I'm ringing up Miss Frazer myself about Alison staying away," she said. "The note is a private one for the head girl, and it's to be given to her personally. You should be ashamed not to be willing to do a little thing like that for your sister when she's not well," she added reprovingly. "Now hurry up and finish your breakfasts, and then fetch the note."

"We've sort of lost our appetites," Jane answered for them both as they edged carefully round the door. "And we haven't much time. It's going to be an awfully busy day."

"'Conscience does make cowards of us all'," their father quoted pointedly, as he folded his paper, preparatory to leaving for his office.

His wife looked perturbed. "You mean you think they're up to some mischief?" she inquired anxiously.

Her husband smiled. "On the contrary, I have my suspicions that we're in for one of their remorseful spells," he predicted darkly.

Mrs. Carstairs sighed. The twins' occasional periods of helpful reform were not always the times of relaxation for their family that one might expect them to be.

CHAPTER EIGHT

TOO MANY COOKS

"ALISON was pleased with the chocolate, wasn't she?" Gillian said with satisfaction, as shortly afterwards, against regulations, she and her twin ran along the road towards school.

Jane nodded. "Yes," she panted. "She smiled, so I should think she's forgiven us about the bike. I meant to ask her about giving the note to Shirley instead of Helen, but she looked so queer I couldn't. She must be very bad to look like that."

"I can't run any more," Gillian announced breathlessly.

"We *must*. Alison said she wanted Helen to have the note as soon as possible," Jane grunted beside her. "I expect it's something to do with her duties."

Helen was in the prefects' room arranging the morning's duties with her helpers, when, after a timid tap at the door, the twins bashfully crept in. There was an interested silence when they appeared. It was an unheard-of thing for those two juniors to present themselves in that room unless under unhappy compulsion. Trying not to notice the awe-inspiring assembly, Jane shuffled forward and presented the note to Helen.

"Thank you," said Helen, smiling at them both. "Is there an answer?"

"I don't know," Jane replied, changing her weight awkwardly from one foot to the other.

"I'd better read it then," Helen said. She scanned the note, then turned a sympathetic face to the twins. "So Alison is ill. She doesn't say what's wrong. I hope it's nothing serious?"

"Oh, yes!" Jane answered with earnest conviction. "She's pretty bad. Mummy thinks she might be having bronokosis and ammonia."

There was a suspicious smothered sound from one of the junior prefects, who turned hurriedly away.

"I think you must mean bronchitis and pneumonia," Helen quietly suggested. The twins nodded solemnly. "I hope it's not as bad as that. I'd like to send Alison a note to stop her worrying," she went on. "Perhaps you'll call for it after school and take it for me, please."

"We—ll, yes," Jane answered grudgingly, in her anxiety quite forgetting whom she was addressing. "If you'll have it *quite* ready for us. We can't *wait* for it, because we said we'd hurry home. We've got to cook the lunch and look after Alison, you see."

There was a stunned silence.

Helen eyed Jane keenly. It was plain that the younger girl *meant* no impertinence. "I see," she said slowly. "Then I must have the note ready by break-time, if you'll come for it then, please."

"Rather odd, isn't it?" Helen remarked when the two juniors had thankfully retreated. "If Alison is as ill as the twins suggest it's strange if they have to cook the meal and look after her. Surely they're not alone. Do you know anything of it, Shirley?"

"I don't," Shirley rather worriedly answered. "But I'll find out. I'll call there on my way home and let you know."

"Thanks," said Helen. "And perhaps you'll deal with any House matters which arise, Shirley. We'd better hurry and get down to our duties now," she added, " or the school will be in an uproar."

" I'm glad you've come," Mrs. Carstairs exclaimed in harassed tones when Shirley arrived at the door later that morning. " Have you seen the twins? They promised to hurry straight home. It's half past twelve. Their father will be coming for me any moment, and I can't leave Alison on her own."

" They're on their way home," Shirley answered comfortingly. " I passed them on my bicycle a few minutes ago. Don't worry, I'll stay with Alison until they get here. Is she very ill?"

" Very ill?" Mrs. Carstairs looked bewildered.

Shirley told her what the twins had said. " *Really*," said their mother. " I never knew such a pair for getting things wrong. I said she must stay in bed to *avoid* bronchitis or pneumonia. She has a bad chill and is feeling most unwell, but I hope she'll be better in a few days. You can pop up and see her for a moment if you like. It's the lunch that's worrying me. I wish the twins would come, so that I could tell them what to do."

" Tell me. I'll see to it," said Shirley practically.

" Thank you, dear," Mrs. Carstairs untied the string of her apron. " The vegetables only need boiling. I've mixed the white sauce for the cauliflower, and the cornflour for Alison. It's all she wants, she says. I can't see how the twins *can* go wrong with anything."

" Who *says* we're going to do anything wrong?" Jane truculently demanded, bursting into the kitchen at that moment. " It's Miss Pearcy who made us late, arguing about some silly island which got itself in the wrong ocean on my map," she grumbled. " Might happen to anybody." She caught sight of Shirley peering into one of the saucepans, and looked none too pleased. " I thought *we* were cooking the lunch," she said indignantly.

" So you are," Shirley answered soothingly. " Your mother was only letting me know what to tell you when you came."

" The trouble is, nobody *trusts* us," Jane muttered huffily, as she in her turn peered into all the saucepans. " Expecting us to do everything wrong. How *can* we when there's nothing to do but light the gas and boil things? Anybody'd think we were *babies*!"

Shirley just grinned as she opened the door leading to the stairs and the invalid. She was still smiling to herself when she entered Alison's room. " I've just been kicked out of your kitchen," she amusedly informed her friend. " The twins have taken charge. How are you, old thing?" she asked with a change of tone. " You look pretty groggy."

" Feel it, too," Alison answered thickly with a weak grin. " Sorry to drop you in for things. But I'll be as fit as a fiddle in a day or two."

" Good," said Shirley. She had missed her friend badly that morning. " But take care and don't rush things," she added teasingly. " Or you may be down with bronokosis and ammonia."

" What's that?" Alison asked densely.

Shirley told her, and they laughed together. " Funny kids," their sister commented affectionately. " They usually *mean* well."

" The skipper sent this note," Shirley said, producing it. " I told the twins I'd bring it as they're so frightfully busy," she added with a chuckle.

" Helen's a jolly good sort," Alison remarked when she had read the note. " We're lucky to have her as head. She thought I might be agitated about not getting our suggestions before Miss Frazer to-day. She says she'll keep an eye on things, and give a hint if necessary."

" Good," Shirley answered. " I'd better be off or I'll be in my mother's bad books. I'll call on my way to the match to see whether the twins have blown the house up."

The maligned pair were at that moment hovering anxiously around the gas stove.

" I can't think why grown-ups make such a fuss about cooking," Jane remarked. " Everything's going beautifully. I wish Mummy had given us something more interesting to cook than prunes for second course. They're so *ordinary*."

" She thought they'd be easy, I suppose," Gillian answered, hitting on the truth.

" Cold meat, too," Jane grumbled. " As if we couldn't cook anything. They don't *trust* us to cook anything, that's what it is. Anyway, it's no use standing and looking at the things. Watched pots never boil, they say. Ours *boil* all right but they take an awful long time cooking. I'm famished. Like Tarzan, I shall start gnawing the meat off the bone if we stand looking at it much longer."

" Good," said Jane a quarter of an hour later, as she prodded viciously at the potatoes. " The vegetables are done." She plucked a piece of cauliflower from its saucepan then nibbled it experimentally. " Tastes just like cauliflower," she said in apparent surprise. " We must be good cooks. Now you make the white sauce for it in that saucepan, and I'll do Alison's corn-flour on this other gas."

" They look super, don't they?" she declared in flushed triumph a few moments later as they peered into each other's saucepans. Now I'll fetch a nice bowl to put Alison's stuff in while you get our lunch set out."

She chased off, and came back with a small bowl, which she hastily filled from a saucepan on the stove.

Gillian looked shocked when she saw the bowl. " But that's one of Mummy's *best* service," she protested. " You know we're not allowed to touch it."

Jane glared at her. " You should always give invalids their food in *pretty* things," she said severely. " They told us that in Guides. It makes them more hungry—the invalids, I mean."

She put the bowl on Alison's tray in dignified silence, and marched upstairs with it.

" *There*," she said proudly, lowering the tray with a bump on to her sister's sore chest. " I made it myself. It should stick you together again, and make you feel better. It's awf'lly gluey stuff."

She proceeded to give her sister's pillow a violent thump or two, sending stabs of pain through Alison's aching head. " There, that's made you more comfortable. Anything else you want?" Jane asked, hovering solicitously over the patient.

" No, thank you very much," Alison answered. " The food looks quite nice," she added thoughtfully.

Jane beamed with pleasure. "Bang on the floor if you want us," she said kindly, opening the door. "We're going to have our lunch now, but we'll hear you."

She hastened down to the dining-room, conscious of an empty vacuum inside her. Gillian was placing the vegetables on the table. Jane sniffed. "Queer smell somewhere," she remarked. "They weren't burnt, were they?"

"Of *course* not," Gillian answered in hurt tones. Then she, too, paused and sniffed. With one thought in mind the twins made a wild dash for the kitchen. Smoke rose thickly from the one remaining saucepan on the gas stove.

"Our *prunes*," Jane cried, grabbing wildly at the saucepan and dropping it quicker than she intended into the sink. "It's hot," she said unnecessarily. Clouds of steam rose as she turned on the cold tap.

They gazed mournfully into the saucepan. A sticky, black mess adhered firmly to the bottom of it, but that was all.

"They were all right when I went upstairs," Jane wailed.

"I—I know," Gillian agreed sadly. "I didn't touch them."

"Well, we can't use them now. I hope the saucepan hasn't a hole in it. Anyway, we've got the other stuff," Jane added philosophically. "We'd better eat that before it gets cold."

A little subdued, they returned to the dining-room, and looked with satisfaction at the substantial helpings of meat and vegetables to which they had treated themselves.

"Sauce?" Gillian asked politely, passing it over.

"Yes, thanks. I like a lot," Jane answered, smothering her plate with it.

Upstairs Alison looked doubtfully at her uninteresting lunch. She was not hungry. "I'd better tackle it," she thought, " or Jane will be mortally offended."

She took a spoonful, and shuddered. Jane had said it looked like glue, and it certainly tasted like it, or perhaps more like paperhangers' paste. The twins had apparently missed the sugar out of it, if nothing else, and there was a queer, salty tang about it. Alison hesitated. It was either her stomach or Jane's feelings which had to suffer. She paused, and then tackled the concoction manfully. There was no point in lingering over it.

She lay very still afterwards, hoping that the twins' cookery effort would settle itself in time. There was a clatter on the stairs. The door burst open, and a pair of wild-looking twins almost fell into the room. Jane rushed to the side of the bed and stared disappointedly into the empty bowl, before looking accusingly at the patient.

"*You've eaten all our white sauce,*" she declared indignantly. Alison roused herself.

"I—I'm sorry," she said, a little densely because of the muzziness in her head. "Sh—shouldn't I have done?"

"Of *course* not," Jane said sternly. "We got the saucepans mixed up. And—and our meat and things are absolutely *drowned* in cornflour pudding," she complained. "We—we *like* white sauce."

"It was jolly good white sauce, too," Gillian complained sadly. "It must have been if you've eaten it all up."

"I—I'm sorry," Alison repeated rather shakily, endeavouring to control her mirth. "Sh—shall I come and get you something else if you can't eat your lunch?" she offered.

"*You haven't to get out of bed,*" Jane ordered sternly. "We promised Mummy. Of *course* we can eat our lunch. We're so hungry we could eat an—an *elephant*. We've p'raps invented a dish everybody'll be wanting to cook soon," she announced hopefully as they hastily retreated downstairs.

Alison hid her face in her pillow; her shoulders shook.

"Not too bad. I feel a bit fuller now," Jane observed a little later. "But there's still plenty of room. We could do with those prunes." She looked pensive for a moment. "I know," she jumped up quickly from her chair. "We'll make pancakes. I know how Mummy does them, and they're awf'lly filling."

"Are you sure? Sure you can do them, I mean?" Gillian protested. "I don't think they're easy to make. You have to keep beating them."

"You only put the egg into the middle of the flour, and keep hitting it, and putting milk in," Jane said easily. "You can hit it twenty times, and I'll do twenty, and I guess it'll look all right."

Strangely enough, even with this rough method, in a short

while the twins had a quite presentable batter mixed together.

"There," said Jane, when they had heated the fat and poured some batter into the pan in the approved manner. "It's sizzling nicely. It smells lovely, too. I've *always* wanted to toss a pancake. I watched them on television, and it looked great fun."

"*Can* you?" Gillian asked anxiously.

"Of course," Jane answered confidently. "We catch balls at cricket, don't we? You can have first try, if you like," she offered generously. "It's ready now."

Gillian made one or two feeble attempts, but the pancake persisted in falling back on to the cooked side. Jane impatiently pushed her away from the pan. "You're being too *gentle*," she said. "You should throw them right up in the air. Like *this*," she demonstrated. Grasping the pan in one hand, she threw the pancake up with a violent jerk and stood waiting with outstretched pan for it to fall back into it. But it did not arrive. Jane's jaw dropped as they both glanced around. There was no sign of it. Gillian looked in bewilderment upwards, as though she expected it still to be floating about.

Then Jane lifted her eyes heavenwards. "Gosh!" she exclaimed. In horror she stared up at the ceiling to which had been added by way of decoration a round ball of half-cooked dough. "Gosh!" she repeated softly, still peering ceilingwards with fascinated eyes.

As usual it was Gillian who had the first qualms. "What shall we do?" she asked shakily.

Jane still gazed raptly upwards, studying her work with the air of an artist. "You know, that took some doing," she observed smugly. "Making it stick up there with its undone side, when you couldn't even turn it over in the pan that way."

"But what shall we *do*?" Gillian repeated agitatedly. "Mummy'll soon be here, and she can't find it stuck up there."

Jane came suddenly down to earth. "We'd better get a long stick or—or something," she suggested. "And stand on a chair and poke at it. It's a pity," she added regretfully, "'cause it looks rather—well, *interesting* up there."

But Gillian had already gone for the stick. She returned, and, dragging up a chair, climbed on it. She poked upwards, but the ceiling was high, and she could not easily reach the pancake, even with the stick. Jane held the chair and watched her, at the same time giving confused instructions.

Gillian at length made a forceful lunge at the pancake. There was a squelching sound as it was dislodged, and a muffled yell from Jane as it landed, uncooked side, on her upturned face.

The door opened. "I'm just popping up to Alison again. How did the cooking go?" Shirley inquired cheerfully, then she stood and stared.

At first she could not see which twin it was who was struggling frantically to free herself from the oozy mass of half-cooked batter completely enveloping her face. Staggering about, almost blinded, Jane was grabbing at handfuls of pancake.

Shirley hastily put down her parcels, and taking the victim by the arm, led her towards the sink.

Gillian slowly descended from the chair, her eyes filling with despondent tears as she gazed round the disordered kitchen. Lumps of hastily discarded batter were everywhere, and there was a round greasy patch on the ceiling.

Jane emerged damply from Shirley's vigorous cleansing. "It tasted like jolly good pancake," she gasped when she had recovered enough breath.

"What on earth you've been up to, I don't know," Shirley exclaimed, staring around in horror. "And it's not my business to find out. But I'd advise you to clean up this place a bit before your parents get back."

"B—but we can't get the mark off the ceiling," Gillian wailed. "We can't *reach*. And—and it's only just been freshly painted. Daddy'll be *furious*!"

Shirley looked upwards in excusable surprise. "How the——?" she began. But she could not waste time on inquiries. "Did you say it was *painted*?" she asked. The twins nodded. "Then fetch me the cobweb brush quickly."

Gillian rushed to obey while Shirley ran some hot water into the washing-up bowl, and hastily shook in some soap powder. She took the long-handled brush which Gillian brought, and climbed on to a chair. "Now hold that bowl for me, please," she said.

She brushed vigorously at the sticky patch on the ceiling. Being taller than the twins she could reach fairly easily. The greasy patch gradually vanished.

"There!" Shirley said with satisfaction, climbing down from the chair. "It's a good thing it was paint and not distemper, or we couldn't have managed it. That's all I can help you with, I'm afraid, so you'll have to scurry round. I'm due on the school field," she said, making for the door. "I shall be in Jean's bad books, as it is. I'll just dash upstairs with these grapes to ease Alison's throat," she added, picking up one of the parcels. Before closing the door behind her she added with a teasing smile, "That other bag is for you two—to help fill up the hole meant for the prunes." Even in her hurry she had not missed seeing the burnt mass in the sink.

Jane rushed towards the remaining bag. "*Scrumptious*," she announced, "It's ice cream. Shirley's a sport, even if she does natter at us sometimes." She closed the bag and put it firmly in the refrigerator. "No, not until we've cleared up the mess here," she told her still hungry twin. "We don't want Mummy to get the silly idea that she can't trust us to cook a meal."

CHAPTER NINE

AN INTERVIEW WITH THE HEADMISTRESS

IT WAS over a fortnight before Alison's doctor allowed her to return to school. She was surprised at the warm welcome she received when she reappeared in the school prefects' room. Even Brenda gave a small grunt of approval. It was not until Alison was relaxing with Shirley over their morning milk and biscuits that she heard the reason for it.

"I'm glad you're back," Shirley told her earnestly. "I could have howled with relief when you reported for duty."

Alison lowered her milk to look at her in surprise. "Why?" she asked. "I haven't been away long."

"Long enough for me to know that I'm not cut out for running the House," Shirley replied gloomily. "I've made a proper mess of it."

"Why? What's wrong?" Alison demanded anxiously. "Who's been playing up? The twins?"

"No," Shirley answered. "Actually they've been surprisingly good for them."

"Well?" Alison pressed.

"Oh, it's just been everything," Shirley said disgustedly. "The House needs a firmer hand than mine. Our Middle Schoolers seem to have gone mad, and Brenda has been at her worst for tactless interfering. She and Rita have bickered most of the time. I suppose you know that Rita has been appointed as school prefect."

"Yes, Helen told me when she came to see me," Alison replied.

"It's the Fifth Formers in our House they've been rowing about. And really," Shirley admitted, "I'm not surprised that Brenda and the seniors in other Houses get a bit peeved. Some of our Fifth Formers are the limit. They've been going about the town in the evenings, acting wildly, and letting the school down. There's nothing one can do about it, either. Goodness knows when they do their prep."

"Ah," said Alison thoughtfully, giving a quick glance at her watch.

"We couldn't tell Brenda or the others that we have something in hand," Shirley went on. "We haven't mentioned it to anyone. When do you think you can do something about it?" she asked anxiously.

Alison put down her empty milk beaker with a thud. "*Now*," she said firmly, turning towards the door.

Shirley stared after her; she was often left a little breathless by Alison's quick decisions. "Now?" she gasped. "But the lesson bell will be going at any moment."

"Plenty of time for making an appointment with the Head for later on," Alison replied decidedly.

"I've fixed an interview with Miss Frazer for this afternoon," she announced to her House prefects after school that morning.

The others gave a sigh of relief. The last fortnight had been a strain.

"I gather that you are still in agreement with the lock-up suggestion?" Alison asked quietly.

"Absolutely," Rita answered immediately. "I've learnt a lot this last week since I've been a school prefect, and seen how our House stands in the eyes of the seniors from other Houses. They've a pretty poor opinion of us, it's plain, though they're too polite to say so openly. Something must be done, even if we do lose a bit of freedom. It won't affect my evening outings for a time, anyway. Miss Frazer's been nattering at me about my maths, and I've to put in extra time at them. Shan't have a minute to spare for gadding about."

"Same here," said Pauline. She hesitated. "You see," she shly revealed, "Miss Frazer wants me to enter for the Pendleton scholarship, and my parents say I may."

They stared at her. "The *Pendleton*," they breathed. They eyed her with amazed respect.

"Goodness," said Rita, almost in awe. "You must have some brains. Nobody from the school has won that scholarship for donkey's years. It's open to a big district, isn't it?"

"Yes," Pauline agreed rather nervously. "I—I don't know why the Head's entering me," she added modestly. "There's not much chance for me, I know, but Miss Frazer thinks it will give me experience for my next exam in July."

"Congrats," Alison sincerely said. "It's an honour for the House for you to be chosen. Is anyone else from the school going up for it, do you know?"

"Yes," Pauline answered. "June Davis from Merton House."

Rita gave a little chuckle. "My word," she said. "*Brenda's* house. Mind you beat June at it. Wouldn't poor old Brenda's hair stand on end if we could get that coveted honour for *our* House."

Joyce spoke thoughtfully. "I think you're wrong about Brenda," she said. "She's very loyal. Her concern is more for the school than for her House, which, I think, is the reason for her attitude towards us. She feels that our House is lowering the school's prestige."

" With which, as I have said before, I quite agree," Alison put in quickly to stem a retort from Rita. " To get back to the original subject," she added, looking round on her helpers, " I'd like to say that I'm grateful to you all for backing me so loyally. It'll be a great help to be able to tell the Head that you're solidly behind me."

Alison cycled home with a lighter heart than she had had for a while. But once she was back at school, and the interview with the Principal loomed nearer, she began to have serious qualms. Would Miss Frazer think she was presumptuous in offering suggestions for the running of the school? Suppose she was angry, and put the whole thing down as an impertinence coming from a House which already stood low in her esteem.

By the time four o'clock came Alison had worked herself up to a fine state of nerves. Her legs felt like water as she tapped at the Principal's sitting-room door. She found herself a little soothed by the cosy atmosphere awaiting her in the room. The Principal sat in a comfortable chair by a cheerful fire, a daintily set tea-table at her side. She greeted the prefect with a welcoming smile.

" Ah, there you are," she said. " Come and sit on this other chair near the fire. I expect you're surprised that I'm spoiling myself with a large fire so early in the autumn," she said as Alison slipped into the comfortable chair offered her. " But I make the excuse that it's because of my age," she added humorously. " After all, it's the only excuse I can think of for it," she finished with a little laugh.

Alison smiled back at her; it was all nonsense, she knew. Miss Frazer was the last person one would connect with advancing age. Her brow was smooth and serene, and her eyes keen and wise as she glanced at the Sixth Former's serious face. She turned to the tea-table, satisfied that she had broken some of the tension which had been apparent when the senior entered the room.

" I thought we'd have a cup of tea before we start on anything else," she said. " Strangely enough, when I received your message from my secretary asking for an appointment I was just on the point of asking her to fix up one with you. So it looks as though it might be a long session. We might as well relax and refresh ourselves first. I've rung up your mother and told her that you may be a little late home, so there's no need to worry on that score," she finished easily as she passed Alison her cup, and offered a plate of dainty sandwiches.

Alison accepted one, and tried to forget the nervous lump which kept rising in her throat.

"Did Pauline tell you that she's entering for the Pendleton scholarship?" Miss Frazer asked.

"Yes," Alison said. "She told us this morning."

"It's a prize which is keenly contested," the Principal went on. "So I dare not raise her hopes too much. Pauline has a very good brain, but she lacks confidence. She has a chance, her knowledge of English Literature is above average." Miss Frazer's face lit up. "If she could top the list, or come near it, it would be a great honour for the school. *And* for your House," she added teasingly.

Alison smiled. "Yes, so Rita has been telling her," she said.

"Ah, *Rita*," the Principal said thoughtfully. She hesitated, and seemed about to speak, but apparently decided against it. Instead, she suggested companionably. "Have one of these little cakes. My help, Ada, made them. I shall get into trouble with her if we don't dispose of a good proportion of them."

Alison did her best, but the time came when the table was pushed aside, and they settled down to more serious things.

"I think we'll have your difficulty first, and leave mine for the moment," Miss Frazer said encouragingly. "We can tackle that better when your mind is more at rest. I can see that you're worried about something. How can I help you?"

Alison gulped. "It—it's about our House," she began falteringly. "I—we, the House prefects, feel that our House isn't pulling its weight. Some of it's our own fault, I suppose. We feel we ought to do something to help build ourselves up to the standard of the other Houses."

"In discipline, do you mean?" the headmistress suggested quietly.

"Mainly," Alison answered. "The chief trouble is discipline, especially amongst the Upper Middles, and a few first year seniors. We can cope with the younger girls. I'm trying to tighten up discipline there. With the older girls it's difficult. The prefects say that they've been troublesome while I've been away. But we don't know what to do about it; our hands are tied in some ways," Alison continued huskily. "Yet we feel that something must be done."

Miss Frazer listened to it all in silence. "In what way do you think I can help you?" she asked quietly.

Alison rather shakily produced the list. "We've talked it over, and—and these are the suggestions which were made," she said, passing it over. "But, of course, we can't do anything about them without help."

Miss Frazer leaned back in her chair and studied the list closely. Watching her anxiously Alison noticed an odd look pass across the Principal's face, rather like the strange expression she had seen in Helen's eyes when she first saw the list, though there was also a hint of displeasure in the set of the Principal's lips.

Miss Frazer lowered the paper and sat up straight. "Yes," she said thoughtfully. She looked keenly at Alison, and seemed to be choosing her words with care.

"I'm interested to know whose ideas these are," she said.

Alison was surprised at her tone. For the moment, the Principal's friendliness had vanished. "The—the House prefects'," she faltered.

"I mean in particular the proposal about lock-up time," Miss Frazer went on in the same expressionless voice.

"Th—that was my suggestion," Alison confessed, feeling that her fears of the afternoon were about to be realised with the wrath of the Principal descending on her head. "I—I'm sorry if you're vexed about it," she said. "I expect it sounds presumptuous to you. But you mustn't blame the others. I thought it out during the holidays, and—and rather pressed it on them."

"Oh," there was a slight lessening in the tension of the Principal's voice. "And who else knows of these suggestions?" she asked.

"Nobody but the House prefects and—and Helen," Alison answered unhappily.

"*Helen!*" Miss Frazer exclaimed rather sharply. "When did *she* know of them?"

"The night I was taken ill," Alison answered in bewildered tones.

There was a short silence. "And what was Helen's reaction to the lock-up suggestion?" Miss Frazer insisted quietly.

Alison struggled to think back. "She seemed surprised, and —and rather odd about it at first, I think," she said. "She asked if we were all agreed on the proposals, and then suggested that I should bring them to you instead of putting them before the school council."

"And that is all?"

"I think so," Alison answered slowly. She looked up at her headmistress. "I—I don't quite understand," she faltered confusedly. "I didn't mean to make you angry with Helen or anything."

"I'm not angry with anyone," Miss Frazer assured her. "I'm very glad you came to me. I was a little concerned, that is all. To ease your mind I'd better explain." Her eyes met Alison's puzzled ones. "It's the coincidence of this which startled me. You have come here with suggestions which are almost identical with some of my own which I had expected to discuss with you in a few moments."

Alison's eyes were wide with surprise. Noticing it, the Principal's last shreds of suspicion vanished. "It seemed so odd," she said, "because though I've had my own plans in hand for improving your House for some weeks, they have, as far as I know, not been discussed with anyone but the staff and Helen, who were all asked not to mention the matter until it became official. I hardly thought that any of my staff or Helen could have betrayed my confidence."

"Oh, no, she didn't, Helen, I mean," Alison answered quickly. "She would never do that. We didn't know that you were doing anything about it. At least," Alison corrected herself, meeting Miss Frazer's eyes frankly, "we didn't know that you had planned anything, but as our House was behaving so badly we expected that you might feel that you should. We thought our suggestions might make it easier."

" They certainly have," Miss Frazer said.

She read the paper again carefully. " You say that all of these suggestions have been passed by your prefects?"

" Yes," Alison answered respectfully. " They said I could tell you that they were in full agreement."

Miss Frazer's eyebrows went up a little. " On *all* of them? The lock-up question? Even Rita?" she suggested.

" Yes."

The Principal's voice was soft. " Then I must say that I am more than pleased," she said. " You are clearly the person your House was needing. I'm delighted that Rita is backing you so loyally. I think you'll find her a great help in the House. I understand that she's already doing good work with the games."

" Yes," said Alison. " Jean's quite pleased." She was wondering whether the headmistress ever missed anything that went on in the school.

Miss Frazer turned to the list again. " These proposals for a name and special badge for your House are quite good. I think there'll be no difficulty in getting both of those passed," she said. " In the matter of lock-up for the day girls, I'll admit that I already had a proposal similar to yours to put before the committee. It shouldn't be necessary if parents would take their responsibilities more seriously. Appeals have failed, so there's nothing to be done but enforce the rule. We can't have matters going on as they are now with the girls bringing discredit on the school. Once the rule is made, if the girls defy it I can act. As you said earlier, our hands are tied at present."

She paused and considered for a few moments. " I think I'll scrap my ideas and put forward your proposals at the Trustee's Meeting," she then said slowly. " You say your House prefects are in complete agreement over them, so I think it would be more encouraging to you to accept them as they stand."

Alison swallowed. " Thank you," she said. " Do you think the committee will agree to the lock-up rule?" she ventured.

" They certainly will," Miss Frazer said. " We all feel that something drastic must be done to keep up the good name of the school. If the parents do not like the rule they must turn their interests to another school. I've a long waiting list of girls who are anxious to enter our school, whatever the rules may be. That brings me to another point," the Principal said. "I suppose you and your prefects realise that if this proposal of yours is accepted by the Trustees it will probably mean a difficult time for you with some of your House?"

Alison looked surprised. "We hadn't thought of that," she confessed.

Miss Frazer smiled. "So I gathered," she said. "If you are in need of support I shall be ready to give it."

"Thank you, Miss Frazer," Alison said gratefully. "I dare say we shall be able to face it."

CHAPTER TEN

A BAD START TO THE DAY

THE NEXT DAY Alison informed her prefects of the results of the interview.

"Then you were right, after all," Rita observed generously. "It's a good thing we got our proposals in first, but it was a narrow squeak."

"It certainly was," Alison answered with a little laugh. "From Miss Frazer's expression when she saw the list I had a nasty feeling that the skies were about to fall. It was strange," she observed, "our both arranging to meet each other with the same ideas in mind."

"We shall be pretty unpopular for a time if the Trustees pass the lock-up rule," Pauline said. "Some of the Fifths and Lower Sixth will resent it bitterly."

"I hadn't noticed any special beams of welcome when we arrive anywhere now," Rita remarked dryly. "So we shan't miss them."

It was a few days before half-term when the Principal called together the whole of the day girls, and published the results of the Trustees' meeting. Notices were already in the post for their parents confirming her remarks, she said.

As the headmistress addressed the House, it became plain to the eagerly listening prefects that, except for a few additions and minor alterations, their proposals had been accepted by the Trustees. Miss Frazer did not mention the prefects at all as having had any share in making the changes, but she looked at them with an understanding smile.

Afterwards she spoke privately to the House prefects.

" The committee asked me to thank you for your suggestions and help," she said. " They say that it promises well for your House that it has leaders who put its welfare before their own wishes." And for the first time in her school life Rita received a personal smile of approval from her headmistress.

" Well, now to the fray," Shirley remarked when they left the Principal's study and emerged into the more public part of the school.

But there was not a lot of trouble in the House that first day. Most of the girls were too surprised by the sudden changes to have had time to think things over properly. A sullen silence hung around some of the Upper Middles and a few seniors, and there was a certain amount of low-toned complaint. Mavis Wills of the Upper Fifth, who was one of the chief offenders in the way of late night outings, was heard grumbling fiercely to her bosom friends.

" It's disgusting, treating us like a lot of babies at our age. This school's getting too stuffy for me," she protested. " I shall ask my parents if I can leave."

It was another fortnight before there were serious signs that the new lock-up rule was beginning to irk. The freedom of the long half-term week-end had for a time satisfied the craving for excitement of a few of the day girls.

Mavis was the first to show resentment. For the first time in her life she had come up against firm opposition from her parents. She was their only child, and they had spoilt her. They had been worried about the late hours she had been keeping, therefore they welcomed the new lock-up rule with open arms, and they refused to do anything to free Mavis from it. The result was that she was feeling thoroughly at odds with everyone.

The twins also chose that time to add to their sister's worries as head of the House.

"We shall be late if you don't get up," Gillian warned her twin when she returned to their bedroom from the bathroom one gloomy November morning.

Jane's eyes appeared far enough above the sheet for her to glare out of the window at the pouring rain.

"Children shouldn't have to go to school on filthy days like this," she complained disgustedly. "No games, no hockey, nor anything decent. There ought to be a law against it," she muttered morosely as she disappeared under the bedclothes again.

There were a few moments of silence, then Jane's nose was again suddenly thrust above the sheets.

"*Somebody's* been pinching Mummy's bath cubes," she stated accusingly with a suspicious sniff.

Gillian looked hurt. "I *didn't* pinch one," she answered indignantly. "Mummy gave it to me when I tidied her drawer for her. Anyway *you'd* want to use something smelling nice if you'd had that beastly oil rubbed on you every night. It's a waste of money, anyway," she added gloomily. "I'll never do the exercises right for Miss Preston. We shan't have any money saved for Christmas presents, either, if we keep on spending it on oil. Christmas is only another month now."

"Goodness, so it is," said Jane, gazing thoughtfully at the ceiling.

"I do wish you'd get up," Gillian said. "We've already been late once this week. We shall be reported if it happens again. Brenda was cross enough last time."

"Brenda's *always* cross," Jane answered definitely. "But I shouldn't worry, it won't be her to-day," she added easily, still making no effort to rise.

"How do you know?" Gillian inquired interestedly.

"Easy, my dear Watson," Jane quoted incorrectly with a grin. "Those school pres have a system. I think I should make a good sleuth if I wasn't going to be a vet. They don't think we kids notice. There's never the same pre on duty in one place more than one day. So if Brenda was on hall duty on Tuesday, when we were late, she won't be there again to-day as it's only Thursday."

Gillian looked doubtful as she fixed her tie carefully. " It might be somebody just as bad as her," she protested.

" There *isn't* anybody as bad," Jane vehemently retorted.

" It might even be Helen," Gillian suggested nervously.

" Oh, it won't be her," Jane asserted confidently. " I've found that out, too. The head girl *never* takes outside hall duty. She has to help Miss Frazer with prayers."

Gillian still looked doubtful. From experience she knew that Jane's theories did not always work out quite the same in fact.

There was a rap on the door. " Hurry up, you two," Alison called. She did not stop to look into the room. They heard her footsteps fading away downstairs.

Jane stretched herself lazily. " S'funny," she observed. " Us being twins. We're not a bit alike. I don't mind an occasional row. It livens things up a bit. We've been so good lately it's been awfully boring. But you're just the opposite. You worry yourself to fiddlestrings about things. No wonder you're skinny."

" I'm *not* skinny," Gillian indignantly answered. " My legs are getting quite fat. They burst my knicker elastic yesterday."

In sudden interest Jane shot up in bed and put her feet on the ground without realising it. " Goodness," she said, gazing at her sister's lower limbs. " *So* they are. It must be all that oil."

Despite Gillian's efforts, breakfast was half over before she and her twin arrived downstairs. They tackled their breakfast enthusiastically and tried to make up for lost time in the way of food. Mrs. Carstairs was enjoying her last cup of tea, and quietly planning her duties of the day, and Alison had already departed for school when sudden piercing yells and shrieks from the kitchen regions brought the family to their feet in alarm. With one accord they left the table and rushed in that direction.

Mrs. Tompkins, their daily help, stood on a chair in the corner of the kitchen, her skirts held tightly around her and with mouth wide open as she uttered terrified, intermittent screams. " Rats! *Black rats*," she shrieked. They came down the chimney and rushed at me, and th—then r—rushed back up again."

The twins were intrigued. Thoughts of school fled from their minds. Mr. Carstairs armed himself with a poker, and watched the chimney intently, while Mrs. Tompkins still stood on the chair emitting occasional squeals. Mrs. Carstairs could not persuade her to descend. There was a rustling sound in the chimney and two small, *very* black animals emerged suddenly and darted across the kitchen. Mr. Carstairs dashed forward with his poker and missed them, though he managed to smash a cup and saucer in his efforts. Pandemonium reigned. Mrs. Tompkins' shrieks reached a crescendo. One small black animal, terrified by the confusion, fled wildly round the kitchen. His luck held, and he finally disappeared through the slightly open kitchen door into the garden. The other little offender had vanished.

After a fruitless search Mrs. Tompkins was eventually persuaded to descend to the floor. It was at this point that Jane announced loudly that they must get off to school. " We'd better feed the animals first, though," she added hurriedly as she edged round the kitchen door.

" But they were *not* rats," they heard their mother assuring the tearful Mrs. Tompkins for the sixth time. " They were *mice*."

Gillian tore after her twin to the shed. Once inside, Jane closed the door and drew her hand carefully out of her pocket. Tenderly, she stroked the terrified little animal in her grasp. Gillian stared at it in amazement. Jane moved over to the cage in the corner, and sighed. " Yes, it *is* them," she said, peering around the empty cage. " They must have chewed their way out. There's a hole in the bottom."

" But they're not ours," Gillian protested. " They're black! Ours are white."

" *Were* white," Jane corrected. " Soot, poor little things. Anybody'd run up the chimney and get sooty with someone screaming at them like that. Mrs. Tompkins ought to be prosecuted for cruelty to animals. It's George we've saved," she went on. " Blossom got away when I opened the door for her."

"*You* opened the door?" Gillian gasped.

Jane grinned. "Of course," she said. "*And* shooed her out, too. Mrs. Tompkins and Mummy didn't notice with all that row going on. We shall have to find her now, Blossom, I mean."

"But what about school?" Gillian said fearfully. "We're late already."

"Yes," Jane answered mournfully, passing a sooty finger over her nose. "I expect we'll have to go. We must look for Blossom at lunch time. We'll put George in this other cage, and clean the soot off him later."

They looked anxiously on the ground as they departed through the garden. There were still sounds of disorder coming from the kitchen, with soothing tones from Mrs. Carstairs in the intervals.

"Silly cowardly thing," Jane said in disgust. "Frightening little helpless animals like that. And I expect Blossom's still out in the rain."

"What if a cat gets her?" Gillian suggested fearfully.

Jane stopped suddenly. "I—I don't think I'll go to school," she gulped. "I'll stay here and watch for her."

"But we *can't* stay at home," Gillian wailed. "We'll get into dreadful trouble."

"That doesn't matter; this is a matter of life and death," Jane moaned. "You can go if you like, but I can't unless I find Blossom."

"I can't go without you," said Gillian. "You—you know we're always in rows together. We'll have another look round."

Fortunately it was not necessary. Jane's anxious eyes were keen. She made a sudden pounce into the bushes as they passed near the kitchen door, and pulled herself upright with another sooty, quivering little animal in her hand. She beamed from ear to ear with relief. "*Both* of them safe," she said joyously. "Now we can go to school and face anything."

They hastily restored the mouse to its lonely mate, and then, ignoring all rules, raced along the road towards the school.

Jane was happy now that their pets were safe, but Gillian was very quiet as they raced along.

"What's wrong?" Jane demanded when they neared the

school and slowed down for safety's sake. "You're not worrying about getting into a row, are you? You needn't. I'll do the talking for us; you know I always do—or, at least," she amended with a grin. "I can usually manage to wear them down a bit before they start on you."

"I—I know," Gillian gulped. "It isn't that. I—I've been thinking about the grown-ups," she confessed. "They—they're so *disappointing*. Daddy and all of them."

Her twin stopped still to stare at her.

"They keep telling us to be kind to animals, and—and everything," Gillian explained. "And then they start waving pokers and things about, and try to m—murder them."

The twins were fond of their father, but Gillian's faith in him was obviously shaken.

"All grown-ups are a bit queer," Jane agreed confidently. "There's that Mrs. Tompkins screaming about the place just because two tiny mice look at her. But I shouldn't worry about Daddy," she added with a broad grin. "He wasn't really trying to catch them, you know, after he saw that they weren't rats. He had to pretend to please Mrs. Tompkins. He winked at Mummy, and he saw me open the door. He was glad they got away, I'm sure."

"Do you really think so?" Gillian said, her faith a little restored. "You don't think Mrs. Tompkins would hurt George and Blossom if she looks in the shed and finds it was them, do you?"

"She won't get in," Jane assured her solemnly. "The shed's locked. Got the key in my pocket," she grinned, with a pat at the spot where it lay. "*Gosh*," she exclaimed in sudden dismay as they hurried up the school drive. "It's *Jean* on duty." Even in her careful calculations she had not reckoned on the school's games captain and second-in-command being the one to deal with latecomers. Jean was an awe-inspiring person, even to the intrepid Jane.

The tall prefect left the spot where she was standing and moved towards the twins. "Well?" she said.

Jane pulled herself together. "I—we're late," she faltered. "M—may we go in to prayers?"

"Certainly not," said Jean. "Prayers are over, anyway. Miss Frazer is talking to the school. They'll be out at any moment. Why are you late? It's the second time this week, isn't it?"

"Yes," Jane agreed meekly, wondering by what means the prefects always managed to learn all these small details. "It was an emergency," she went on earnestly, encouraged by the senior's kindly gaze, so different from Brenda's blustering methods. "It was a matter of life and death," she brought out, enjoying the repetition of the phrase. "George and Blossom might have died if we hadn't waited to save them."

"George?" the games captain repeated, feeling the usual sense of confusion creeping over her when dealing with Jane. "Who are George and—and Blossom?"

"Our white mice. George is the gentleman, and Blossom's his wife," Jane explained. "At least," she amended, "they *were* white mice, but they've turned black—Well, not *really* turned black," Jane corrected herself again. "It was just the soot from the chimney. And, of course, when Blossom——"

Jean stroked her hair in a distracted manner. She had an interview with Miss Frazer before lessons, and if Jane was starting on one of her lengthy explanations— Jean turned in relief towards a doorway in the hall through which the Sixth Form had started to emerge. Shirley was amongst them and, at a sign from Jean, came over.

"These two belong to your House," said Jean, indicating the twins. "I have to see the Head; I'll be glad if you'll take them to your House captain for me. It's the second time they've been late this week, so it means a report. They have some sort of excuse, but I can't work it out." Jean's eyes twinkled as they met Shirley's.

Shirley left the twins outside when the three of them reached the prefects' room. Alison was there, and also a very distressed-looking Ruth. Shirley wondered whether it would be more tactful to withdraw.

"Don't go," Alison told her, noticing her hesitation. "It's nothing private. It's just that—well, what we expect has happened," she said with a little smile. "The news of our share in the lock-up rule has leaked out. Some of Ruth's form are giving her an uncomfortable time."

"Mavis is furious," Ruth faltered. "She and some of the others challenged me about it. I couldn't deny it, of course."

"No need to, we're not ashamed of it. Hard words will hurt none of us," Alison said.

"That's true," Shirley agreed. "But actually I came here to make a report for Jean," she told her friend. "It's the twins; they've missed prayers for the second time this week."

"Oh," Alison answered. "Then I expect I'd better——"

The door opened suddenly. "Well, the mischief is out," Rita proclaimed with a flourish as she entered the room. "Already little groups are gathering together to pull our characters to pieces. We're in for a lively day."

"So it seems," said Alison.

"About the twins——" Shirley reminded her.

Alison passed a hand across her forehead. "Oh, look into it and deal with them for me, please," she said as she moved towards the door. "I must go and move on the people who are standing about gossiping or we shall have Helen and the staff on our track. The lesson bell will be going any minute now."

Shirley sighed. "Then I'd better see the twins at break-time," she answered resignedly. "One needs *time* for Jane's explanations."

She did need time, *and* patience, but at last she got to the bottom of the affair.

"So you see we couldn't *help* being late," Jane finished hopefully.

"I'm not sure of that," Shirley said.

"But we couldn't leave George and Blossom to be hurt, and perhaps m—murdered by a cat or something," Jane protested. "Don't you *like* animals?"

"Yes, I do very much," Shirley answered. "Still——"

"Haven't you *got* any?" Jane broke in.

"No, I haven't," Shirley started again. "But——"

"Not even a cat or dog?" Jane persisted.

"No, not even a cat or dog," the prefect answered patiently. "I wish I had, but that's not the point——"

"*Gosh*," Jane interrupted, overcome with sympathy. "No animals at all, and you *like* them. How *awful*. We'd better save you one of Fluff's kittens when she has some again. They're *beauties*, aren't they, Gill?"

Shirley felt that matters were getting a little out of hand. "Thank you," she said firmly. "But to get back to the point. You admit you were late getting up to-day, and from Brenda's report that seems to have been the excuse the other time you missed prayers this week."

"But not Gill," Jane assured her anxiously. "Gill *never* lies in bed when she shouldn't. It's awkward for her, but her conscience won't let her. She always gets out when she's called."

Shirley looked at Gillian, who hung her head as though ashamed of her weakness. "That's one thing that puzzles me about you two," the prefect said. "Gillian's a sensible person. I can't understand why she always has to be dragged into these affairs."

The two juniors looked at her with shocked eyes. "But we're *twins*," they both protested, Gillian finding her voice for once.

All the same, despite Jane's earnest efforts to keep the senior's mind off the real matter in hand, she arrived there in the end. There was no shirking with Shirley on such occasions. The result was that the twins spent the rest of that morning in a very depressed and disgruntled mood.

CHAPTER ELEVEN

REACTIONS

MATTERS were no better when the twins arrived home for lunch. They raced to the shed to see if their sooty pets were safe before having a hurried wash and presenting themselves breathlessly at the dinner table.

They were not exactly welcomed with open arms. Their mother eyed them suspiciously even when she noticed the clean shining faces and demure air of her two young daughters. This in them she knew of old was usually a sign of a guilty conscience.

She handed them their first portions of food in silence. Jane devoured hers with satisfaction, and speculated on the nature of the second course as she sat with hands meekly folded in her lap waiting for the rest to finish. " It's a nice day now, even if it has been raining, isn't it?" she offered brightly in an effort to ease the tension.

Alison had been deep in thought. She had had a trying morning, but she looked up now, rather surprised at her sister's unusual efforts at polite conversation.

" I—er—yes," she said.

Mrs. Carstairs reached for Jane's plate for a second helping. There was never any need to ask. She looked at Jane sternly.

" *Where are those mice*?" she demanded suddenly.

Jane jumped a little. " M—mice," she said sweetly. " The black ones?"

" Your *white* ones," Mrs. Carstairs said firmly. " Where are they?"

Jane opened innocent eyes. " In the cage in the woodshed," she said.

" Then why was the shed locked this morning?" Mrs. Carstairs demanded. " *And* the key taken?"

Jane hesitated for a moment. " Why? To keep the animals safe, of course," she said, as though surprised at her mother's denseness.

" Meaning they might turn the key in the lock to get out if you left it there, I suppose?" Mr. Carstairs put in dryly from his end of the table.

Jane eyed him reproachfully. " They're awfully intelligent animals," she answered with dignity.

Her father hid his amusement with difficulty. " Come," he said. " You might as well face up to it. *Were* those your animals in the kitchen this morning?"

Jane's look of reproach deepened. " Daddy," she said righteously. " That's not quite fair. You know I can't tell a lie."

Her father blew his nose hurriedly.

" Then did you let them out deliberately to frighten Mrs.

Tompkins?" Mrs. Carstairs demanded sternly. The twins were capable of it, she considered.

Jane's look of horror was sufficient answer. She put her knife down with a clatter. "I—I wouldn't let a—a *fly* into her beastly kitchen if I could help it," she almost shouted. "I think grown-ups are *awful*, yelling and frightening little things like that. Anybody'd think there was a—a rhinoceros in the room."

"Mrs. Tompkins has a phobia about mice," her mother explained.

"She couldn't have with *mice*," Jane said definitely. "That's what you get with dogs when they bite you, and none of our animals bite."

"That's hydrophobia, you silly girl. A phobia means that Mrs. Tompkins is afraid of mice," Mrs. Carstairs told her patiently, beginning to wish that she hadn't started on the subject. "She has been very poorly all the morning," she went on. "She says she won't stay here if your mice get into the kitchen again, and I don't mean to lose her because of your animals. If you can't look after them properly they'll have to go."

"*Mummy!*" The twins pushed aside their plates with a wail. "We couldn't *help* it if they chewed their way out. We *must* have animals. How can I be a vet when I grow up if I don't have animals?" Jane demanded.

"You have too many to see to in term time," said their mother. "Especially when you don't get up in time. I won't have you bringing any more animals home—understand that."

Jane and Gillian were in a thoroughly disgruntled mood when they set out for school again. "It's like you said this morning. Grown-ups are the absolute *edge* sometimes," Jane said fiercely, kicking viciously at a stone as they went along. "Now we must go back to school, and I expect everybody there'll be as cross as two sticks like they were all the morning."

"They certainly *were*," Gillian agreed sadly.

"Who *cares* whether the pres helped to make the lock-up rule," Jane continued to growl. "If that Gloria Gaynot keeps moaning about Alison much more something'll happen," she predicted darkly. "What difference does it make to her? She's only a kid like us, even if she does like to pretend she's grown up. I expect she's caught it off that daft cousin of hers, Mavis Wills, in the Fifth. They're both of them as soppy as they can be."

With Jane in this mood it was surprising that she contained herself for as long as she did. Lessons did not go very well for her that afternoon, either. "That Miss Benson's awfully fussy and—and insulting," she remarked indignantly to her twin when they were on their way to their cloak-room to change for games. "Fancy saying my sewing was disgraceful and *dirty*. How could it be *dirty*? We washed specially well at lunch time. Now I've yards and yards to unpick to-night, as well as piles of prep. We shan't get any time to play. I don't know what's the matter with everyone to-day."

Gillian made sympathetic noises. "If I help you to unpick perhaps we'll get a little game," she offered.

"Thanks. But if there's much more of it I shall *explode*," Jane threatened. "Natter, natter, *natter*! That's all everyone does to-day."

"Who's talking in the corridor?" Brenda demanded, suddenly appearing through one of the doorways.

Jane stopped and stared around in exasperation. "It must be us," she said crossly, "as there's nobody else about."

Brenda fixed her with a prefectly glare. "There's no need to be impertinent," she said. "You can do me fifty lines for your rudeness, and both of you will take an order mark for breaking the rule. The girls in your House seem to have lost their heads entirely to-day," she added unwisely as she turned away. "You are all going out of your way to make yourselves even bigger nuisances than usual."

Jane glared after her. "That's the last bit of to-night's free time gone," she said in a furious whisper. "She's a beast, always pulling our House to pieces. If anybody else says anything about our House to-day I'll—I'll——"

It was unfortunate that at that moment they had to pass a group of Fifth Formers from their House who were conversing in undertones. Amongst them was Mavis Wills, who appeared to be doing most of the talking.

" The House has been unbearable since she was made captain," Mavis was saying. " You can be sure that she bullied the rest of the pres into supporting the lock-up rule. They wouldn't have agreed otherwise. She's nothing but an interfering, bossy upstart."

As Jane and Gillian were hurrying by, aware that they might be late for their games hour, these remarks fell on their ears and brought them to a sharp halt. It was the last straw for Jane.

She rushed up to Mavis, eyes blazing. "How *dare* you call our sister names?" she cried. " She's *decent*. She's worth hundreds of you. It's because of people like you going out at night and letting the House down we have to have the rule."

Mavis's mouth dropped open with shock, and her cronies fell back in surprise. Then, realising that her fiery attacker was only an unimportant member of the junior school, Mavis grabbed Jane by the shoulders and shook her furiously. "You cheeky young imp," she said angrily, punctuating each word with another shake. "How *dare* you speak like that?"

Gillian rushed forward, anxious to assist her twin, but Jane made a sudden lunge with her foot, and with an unexpected twist freed herself, leaving the startled Mavis rubbing her bruised shin.

The twins rushed for the safety of their cloak-room. Expecting retribution to follow them at any moment, they sunk on to their lockers, and shakily started to change into plimsolls. It came, but not from the quarter they expected. The door burst open to admit two excited members of their own form. The despised Gloria was one of them.

"You—you beast," she said, rushing up to Gillian. "Kicking my cousin and laming her. I heard what you said. Your sister *is* bossy, trying to turn the House upside down. She thinks too much of herself."

It was too much for Jane. Still with only one plimsoll on, she flew to her sister's defence. There was a struggle with sundry oh's and ah's and bangs, until five minutes later, more or less worsted, the invaders departed as suddenly as they arrived, leaving Jane with a bleeding nose, hair on end, a torn blouse, and a subdued air.

Her twin tearfully escorted her to one of the washbasins. Jane hung her head over it, and hopefully dabbed at her nose with cold water.

" Sh—shall I get a key from somewhere?" Gillian asked anxiously as the blood continued to flow. " They say that stops it."

Jane shook her head. " No, it'll soon stop, I expect," she answered in muffled tones.

The door opened, unnoticed by them. The tall prefect standing there watched them silently for a moment or two. Then she went over to them. " You're doing the wrong thing," she said quietly. " Sit up and hold your head only slightly forward. That will stop the bleeding more quickly."

Jean fetched a chair, and seating Jane upon it, started to carry out her own advice. The bleeding gradually lessened as she continued to bathe Jane's offending nose with cold water, Jane submitting to it all meekly. For the school games captain to be attending to her needs seemed to be only one more peculiar happening of that unfortunate day.

Jean straightened herself and looked down on them both. " You seem to be making a day of it, don't you?" she said quietly. " I came to find you because I've had a complaint about you. Mavis Wills says she couldn't report to me for games because you, Jane, had kicked and lamed her. Is that true?"

Jane nodded. " I suppose so. I did kick her," she admitted with a gulp.

" But *why* did you kick her?" Jean asked.

Jane's eyes flew open in surprise. " Because I couldn't reach up any farther," she said simply. " You should never hit an enemy in the stomach," she explained.

Jean swallowed hastily. " I mean," she said carefully, " why should you want to hit her at all?"

Jane hesitated. " She—she said things about—someone," she answered.

" What sort of things?"

Jane did not answer. Jean placed another cold pad in place.

"I think I understand," she said. "But surely Mavis didn't knock your nose like this?" she suggested.

"Oh, no! She only shook me," Jane said.

"Then who did it?" Jean asked.

"I—er," Jane faltered. "You see, we had a fight—one of the other juniors and me. I expect she felt she had to do something. We—I—I think we were both fighting for the same thing," she said with sudden enlightenment.

"Loyalty?"

Jane looked at the prefect quickly. Jean's eyes were understanding. "I—I suppose so," she faltered.

The door opened again and Rita strode in. She seemed surprised to see Jean. "I came to find these two," she said, indicating the twins. "They should be at games."

"I think you'll have to excuse them to-day," Jean replied. She passed her own freshly soaked handkerchief to Gillian. "There, carry on with that for a few moments," she told her. "Then I think Jane will be all right."

She drew Rita to the other side of the room, out of earshot. "I'm not sure what to do with these infants," she said. "Mavis Wills had a kick from Jane, and of course I can't uphold juniors attacking seniors. The skipper may think it a school matter, but, frankly, I'm not anxious to send the kids to her just now. She's a bit—well, on the edgy side to-day. She's had nothing but reports of rows and things all day."

Rita gave a wry smile. "It's the same with us," she revealed. "Alison is properly on the war path. We've had a vile day."

Jean smiled at her. "We can guess what it's all about," she said quietly. "But you'll win through. Helen is solidly behind you, as well as myself."

"Thanks," Rita said gruffly. "Shall I take these two kids to Alison, then? I expect she'd rather attend to it than have Helen dragged into it."

"Settled," said Jean. "I'm glad to wash my hands of the affair. Actually I should have been on the field ages ago." Her lips broke into a smile as she glanced across at the subdued twins. "Strictly off the record, though," she said in confidential undertones as she turned to go, "I hope Alison doesn't come down too hard on the infants. I believe even the dauntless Jane has had about enough for to-day."

When Rita arrived at the House prefects' room with the reluctant twins in tow she left them outside the door while she explained the situation to the House captain.

Alison had decided to give up her recreation hour that afternoon to try to catch up with some of her school work. The many hindrances of the day had put her behind with it. It should be quiet up in the little room in the tower if most of the school was out on the playing fields, she decided.

But she was mistaken, for she had one interruption after another.

Ruth left the room as Rita entered it. Alison lifted her eyebrows ruefully at the further interruption. She pushed aside her books. " It seems hopeless to try to study this afternoon," she said. " Ruth has just been in to tell me that Mavis and her crowd have decided to send her to Coventry because of her share in our suggestions. Such infantile nonsense! Only fit for children in nurseries. Of course, it has upset Ruth a bit."

" Be all the better for some of us if they *do* do a little less talking," Rita said dryly. " They need a good shaking. I've a bit of sympathy for Jane's methods."

" Jane?" queried that junior's sister wearily. " What has she been up to now?"

Rita told her.

" I can't see why Jean couldn't have dealt with us herself, if someone's got to," Jane complained as she and her twin waited outside the door. " People keep passing us on to somebody else all day," she grumbled. " Anybody'd think we'd got something *catching*."

" I expect Jean thinks Alison wouldn't want her to interfere in House affairs," Gillian said wisely.

" Then I wish she wouldn't be so finicky about it," Jane replied. " I *like* Jean. S'funny," she said, " Though she's wizard at hockey and bangs the ball like—like anything, her hands were awf'lly gentle when she was bathing my nose."

" Yes," said Gillian. " She's kind. So's Alison really," she added loyally with a nervous glance at the door. " But she's awf'lly strict. She has to be as we are her sisters, I suppose, else the others would think she was favouring us."

" Yes, I expect she'll drop on us like a ton of bricks," Jane agreed sadly. " She'll go into everything, from my getting up late this morning to my banging that Gloria on the head this afternoon. She never misses anything." She eyed her sister oddly. " But you haven't done anything," she said. " You needn't be in it."

Gillian looked shocked. " But we're *twins*," she protested once more. " I couldn't *bear* not to be in everything with you."

As the twins had predicted, Alison was pretty thorough in her handling of the affair. Further penalties were showered on her erring sister, and Alison's remarks were sharp and very much to the point.

" Gloria is to blame for some of it, and I'll see her later," she said. " But I'm tired of having to deal with you. I have one complaint after another about you. If there's much more trouble with you, I shall send you to Helen," she warned the downcast twins firmly. " I won't have the prefects and the rest of the school continually upset by your antics."

CHAPTER TWELVE

JANE'S GOOD TURN GOES AWRY

ALISON would never forget the next two or three weeks. The future of Chester House appeared to be in the balance. It was divided against itself. On one side, Mavis and her allies exerted themselves in an effort to overthrow the rule of the prefects. Opposing them were the leaders of the House and a large majority of their loyal supporters. Alison often wondered during those troublesome weeks which caused her the most worry—her supporters, or her opponents. Her younger adherents were inclined to be over zealous in their loyalty; the twins, of course, amongst them.

After almost three weeks of the struggle, Alison felt that she could stand no more. She was tired out. Brenda's criticisms of her House caught her on the raw more than ever, for she knew that there was good reason for them. Despondency set in. Had she made a mistake in taking on the headship of the House? She even went so far as to suggest to Helen that it might be better for the House if she resigned.

Helen's friendly eyes filled with concern at the proposal. " Of course it wouldn't," she said definitely. " There's no one who could take your place, or do as well as you in controlling the House."

" But I'm making such a mess of things," Alison faltered.

" You're tired and have things out of proportion," Helen answered thoughtfully. " Considering everything, I think you're coping with matters firmly and well, and so does the Head."

Alison looked at her in astonishment. " *Does* she?" she exclaimed.

Helen nodded. " Things will solve themselves in time. Mavis isn't being too discreet in her actions," she said grimly.

Alison looked at her. " You mean——?" she ventured.

" Miss Frazer is almost certain that Mavis is deliberately ignoring the lock-up rule," Helen replied. " She'll overstep herself pretty soon, I'm sure."

" Oh," said Alison. " Then you think I should carry on?"

" I don't think—I *know*," Helen answered with a little laugh.

She was right. When the school assembled after the Christmas holidays, Mavis was missing from Chester House. Because of the anxious pleading of her parents, to Mavis's disgust, she was not removed entirely from the school, but was transferred to Merton House as a boarder. There would be no evading the lock-up rule there.

With her away, the ill feeling in Chester House gradually vanished, and things went more smoothly for a while.

The New Year resolutions the twins had made were forgotten by the time they arrived at school for the new term. They again fell into trouble with appalling regularity. As Jane protested in excuse, they did not *look* for it, it just *happened* to them.

It "happened" once more on a day soon after the term began. The twins were hurrying home to their midday meal when their attention was caught by the protesting squeals of a tiny black and white spaniel. It was being dragged along the pavement by a rough-looking boy. Round the puppy's neck was a piece of string which was tugged viciously each time the puppy lagged behind.

Jane's indignation rose as she and Gillian followed them. The puppy's legs dragged slower and slower until at last it sat down exhausted in the middle of the pavement. Annoyed, the boy tugged at the string until it cut tightly into the little creature's neck, but it did not move. It could not, it was too weary. The boy then gave the puppy a cruel, exasperated kick which made it yelp with pain. Like a whirlwind Jane dropped the books she was carrying and entered the fray. "You cruel bully," she cried.

The boy was much taller than Jane, but she had learnt her lesson about kicking. It was the boy's turn to yelp as her sharp teeth bit the hand which held the string. He let it go in surprise, and the puppy crawled nearer to Jane. The boy was still rubbing his wrist when Jane picked up the small dog. Her eyes blazed with indignation. "I'll—I'll tell the 'Cruelty to Animals' man," she said fiercely, as she stroked the cowering morsel in her arms.

"Can't keep it," the boy muttered in excuse. "Was going to drown it."

Jane glared at him. "To—to *drown* it," she exclaimed in strangled tones, cuddling the puppy closer.

The boy's eyes narrowed as he watched her. "Want to buy it?" he suggested hopefully.

Jane hesitated. Then she thrust her free hand into her pocket. "How much?" she asked.

"Ten bob," the boy suggested eagerly.

"I—I've only got half-a-crown," Jane answered. It was her week's pocket money.

"Then I'll take that," said the boy and, snatching the money from Jane's hand, he rushed down the street and round the next corner, leaving the twins staring stupidly after him.

Gillian moved nearer to stroke the puppy as it snuggled confidently in Jane's arms. "*Now* what do we do?" she asked practically. "All your pocket money's gone, and we can't take the puppy home. You know what Mummy said."

"Goodness," said Jane. She had forgotten her mother's threats.

"She said she'd stop us from having any animals at all if we take any more home," Gillian reminded her.

Jane looked glum. "Pity," she said, rubbing her chin gently against the puppy's silky head. "He's so sweet. We'll have to hide him somewhere while we have our dinner, anyway," she decided.

"I know what we'll do," she exclaimed suddenly a short while later, wiping her none-too-clean hands on a towel in the bathroom. "We'll give him to Shirley. She said she wished she had an animal, and she's an awfully decent sort. It'll be a nice surprise for her," Jane went on, intrigued by the idea. "It's games for the Sixth the last part of the afternoon . . . I'll put it in her locker. She's bound to find it when she goes to change her shoes."

"B—but," Gillian protested anxiously, "we're not allowed to go into the Sixth cloak-room. And—and how do you know which is her locker?"

"I do know," Jane answered with smug satisfaction. "Shirley sent me to fetch something from it last term. No one will see us putting the puppy there if we get back to school early. Anyway, we ought to be willing to take risks about rules to make people happy when we're Guides," she added virtuously. "We haven't done our good deeds for to-day yet, and Shirley'll be awfully thrilled."

Gillian had her doubts about that as she hurried downstairs to dinner.

"It's the last straw!" Brenda almost shouted as she waved the mangled remains of her plimsolls wildly before the eyes of the long suffering head girl, half-way through that afternoon. "If you don't make those twins suffer for it, I shall."

"Of course I shall deal with it when you give me the proper facts," Helen said quietly. "So far," she added dryly, "you've done nothing but shout at me and wave those plimsolls in front of my nose. What actually happened?"

Brenda choked back her anger with an effort. " I went to my locker to change for games," she said in strangled tones, " and a puppy bit me. Somebody had made it a bed on my blazer. My First Eleven one," she raised her voice to emphasise the enormity of the deed. " It had pulled the pocket and badge off it, and chewed all the uppers off my plimsolls, as you see," she said, indicating the wrecks of footwear she had been waving about. " Goodness knows what I'm going to wear on the field. I should be there now."

" You must borrow mine," Helen offered. " I'm not playing to-day. We're the same size, I believe. What makes you suspect the twins?" she inquired.

Brenda coloured hotly as she threw a label on to the head girl's desk. " You'd better read that," she said. " It was tied round the animal's neck with a bow of—of red ribbon," she finished disgustedly.

Helen picked up the label. " WITH LOVE FROM THE TWINS ", she read. Her eyebrows quirked comically.

Brenda fidgeted under the look. " Sarcasm, I suppose," she said bitterly. " There's no love lost between us, as you know."

" No," Helen said slowly. " But it's odd. Somehow I can't connect sarcasm with the twins. Where is the puppy now?" she asked.

" Still in the locker with the top propped open for air, as I found it," Brenda said forcibly.

" Then leave it to me," Helen told her. " You'll find my gym shoes in my locker. Yours are beyond hope, I'm afraid."

Not many minutes afterwards, the twins stood nervously at attention before the head girl's desk. The sight of the puppy on the mat before the fire, blissfully disposing of the remains of Brenda's plimsolls, told them why they had been summoned. It was hardly playing the game for Shirley to have reported them after their efforts on her behalf, they thought resentfully.

" Well," Helen said, " I suppose you admit that you broke rules by bringing an animal to school, and by going into the Sixth Form cloak-room without permission?"

" Y—yes," Jane faltered. She was uncertain about what kind of excuse to make.

" Then what made you do it?" Helen demanded. " Why did you wish to annoy Brenda in that way?"

At that Jane woke up. " *Brenda*?" she exclaimed indignantly. " We haven't done *anything* to Brenda, we haven't wanted to. At least," she added with her usual rambling thirst for honesty, " we might have *felt* that we wanted to, but we haven't, have we, Gill?"

Helen's voice was sterner. " If you say you've done nothing to Brenda, why was the puppy found in her locker?" she asked, " where it had torn her blazer, and chewed her plimsolls to pieces?"

Jane's mouth dropped open. " But it *wasn't* in Brenda's locker, it was in *Shirley's*," she protested. " We put it there as a *present* to her. We shouldn't *think* of giving anything jolly like that to Brenda."

Helen let that pass. " Then it seems that in addition to breaking rules you made a mistake in the locker——" she observed.

" I *couldn't* have done," Jane argued. " I know it was the second from the end."

" It *was*," Helen said dryly. " But it has been changed. Not that that's any excuse for you. You had no right in the room at all, and——"

" But we *had* to be," Jane interrupted again unwisely. " We couldn't let the puppy be drowned. We'd nowhere to *put* him, and——"

Helen endeavoured to speak. " But surely——"

" It was because of the mice which Mrs. Tompkins thought were rats," Jane explained incoherently, speaking quickly, as she usually did when interviews of that kind showed signs of reaching a crisis. " Mummy thinks there are too many about —animals, not mice, I mean," she explained hurriedly in case the head girl might think their house was overrun with vermin. " Ours are tame—the mice, I mean, so are all of the animals. But there are such a lot of them. Not too many for us, of course," she continued hastily, as the head girl opened her mouth in another attempt to check her. " We don't mind *how* many we have, but Mummy does because of Mrs. Tompkins getting screaming fits, and frightening them. We couldn't leave the puppy at home 'cause *something might have happened to it*," Jane revealed darkly, giving the bewildered head girl a confused impression of a house overrun with mice, screaming women, and mysterious people with murderous intentions. "We'd have liked the puppy for ourselves," Jane rambled on, "but it wouldn't have been *safe*, nor for any of the other animals. And we——"

"*Stop*!" Helen thundered suddenly in a voice which even the Sixth Form had learnt to respect.

Jane "stopped" in surprise with her mouth still open. She stared at the grim-looking head girl.

"It's no use trying that sort of rigmarole on me," Helen said sternly. "I've no time for it. Go and stand at the other side of the room until you're ready to listen to what *I* have to say. Yes, right over by the opposite wall," she added, as the shocked twins hesitated. "It'll give you time to think things over quietly," she finished firmly, though in more gentle tones. So saying she turned back to her desk and the papers in which she had been engrossed before Brenda's appearance.

Silence fell on the study, broken only at intervals by the entry of a few seniors who had business with the head girl. They glanced at the twins. To see that troublesome pair standing in so subdued and quiet a fashion was something new to them. Well, if Helen could not manage them nobody could.

The minutes went by, and still Helen wrote diligently at her lists, referring occasionally to the papers at her side. Once or twice she glanced up at the twins, her face expressionless. "Poor little beggars," she thought, hardening her heart with difficulty, especially when she saw Gillian furtively brushing away the tears in her eyes, but she must try to make some lasting impression on the culprits, the head girl decided.

At length a smothered sob from Gillian was too much for her. She glanced at her watch, and pushed aside her papers.

"Come over here now," she said gently.

They came. Helen's mouth softened as she looked at them. Even the redoubtable Jane, who never cried, was by then gulping madly to prevent it. It upset her to see her twin in distress, and her conscience was not too easy about her own share in causing it.

"Dry your eyes and tell me exactly what happened about the puppy, will you, Gillian?" Helen said kindly.

Gillian stopped crying to stare at her in horror. She turned to her twin as though in appeal.

Jane could not ignore her sister's anxious look.

"Gill's nervous about talking," she gulped. "I've always had to do it for her."

"Then she must learn to speak up for herself," Helen said with a smile. "There's no need to be nervous, anyway. I just want the straight tale without any frills, and I know I shall get it from Gillian."

Thus encouraged, Gillian wiped her eyes and told what was necessary, shielding her twin as much as she could.

"So Jane has spent all her week's pocket money on the puppy," Helen remarked when she finished. "Does Shirley know you're giving it to her?"

The twins shook their heads. "Then we'd better catch her and tell her before she goes home," Helen said. "Though I don't know what the position will be. I believe the reason she hasn't had a pet is because she lives in a flat, and pets aren't allowed."

The twins' eyes opened in concern. "Don't worry, I dare say we can fix up something," Helen assured them, with an amused look at the black and white imp of mischief on her mat. "He's too engaging a morsel to be without a home for long." Her voice grew serious again.

"You know, you two have the makings of a very useful pair in the school," she said. "In a year or two your House will be needing you to keep up the standards which your sister is working hard to build up. I've a great respect for Alison, she's doing grand work in your House, but you keep adding to her difficulties. Doesn't it occur to you that you're not supporting her as well as you should?"

For the second time in that interview, the twins looked thoroughly shocked. "But we *do* stick up for her," Jane protested with a gulp. "We've been fighting, and—and everything for her."

"I don't mean that kind of support," Helen answered quietly. "That's the wrong way to go about it. You've worried her a great deal by the scrapes you get into. You can help her a good deal if you try. You're an honest pair, and you in particular, Jane, are a good leader if you'll only *think* a bit more before you do silly things, and drag Gillian into scrapes with you. And you, Gillian——" Helen paused as she looked into that junior's sensitive, clever face. "You're really a sensible, level-headed person. Even if Jane does do mad things, don't let her drag you into them when you don't really approve of what she's doing. Learn to be brave, and stand on your own feet. You'll have to later on, you know. In a few years, the school will be needing you both to take the place of people like Alison and myself. Yes, I mean it," she finished smilingly as the twins stared incredulously at her.

There was more to the interview, of course. Payment had to be made to Brenda for her damaged belongings, which would keep the twins short of pocket money for some time. But it was the head girl's friendly talk which made the most impression on them.

Jane and Gillian arrived home that day in a dazed and thoughtful mood which kept them subdued for days.

"I hadn't really thought of our being two separate people," Jane said soberly as she sat on the edge of her twin's bed that night. "I believe Helen thinks I bully you into getting into scrapes with me. But I don't do I?"

"No—I *like* doing things with you," Gillian owned.

"So do I with you," Jane agreed. "But I suppose Helen's right. You must do what you think yourself. You'll have to, if we might be pres some day like Helen said. It makes my tummy feel funny inside to think of it, doesn't it yours?"

Gillian nodded speechlessly.

There followed a week of blissful calm for everyone as far as the twins were concerned. Their excessive meekness and politeness to their superiors was almost embarrassing. Alison was at first bewildered when the twins eagerly hustled one another for the privilege of carrying her books, or helping her in other small ways. They even spent the whole of their next free Saturday afternoon cleaning her bicycle for her. For days it shone brightly with their elbow grease and good resolutions.

The head girl's efforts to impress them with the importance of their elder sister had not been wasted. The exalted Helen had said she respected and admired her, and that was sufficient for the twins.

CHAPTER THIRTEEN

COMPANY TO TEA

" MAY I bring one of the girls home to tea to-morrow, Mummy?" Alison asked as she finished her breakfast one morning.

"Certainly, dear," her mother replied. "Shirley, do you mean?"

"No, one of the boarders," Alison answered, and the twins pricked up their ears. "She's been very decent to me. I've had tea with her two or three times, and I'd like to return it. I thought she'd enjoy it here more than in a restaurant. The boarders don't get much home life."

"No, poor things," said Mrs. Carstairs, pleased that Alison was bringing home a friend. "We'll get a nice tea for her. It'll be a change from school fare. Is it anyone I know?"

"I think you've met her," Alison answered. "It's Helen Blakely, the head girl."

There was a gasp from the twins. They had been carefully dodging Helen for the last week. The memory of their interview with her still—embarrassed them. "B—but you can't have *her* here," Jane broke out in anguished protest.

Alison looked at her. "Why not?" she demanded.

"Because—well, you *know* you can't," Jane burst out, wriggling uncomfortably. "You *know* we've had a row from her.

We'd feel awf'lly silly, wouldn't we, Gill? It—it isn't *decent*."

Her parents listened to this outburst in astonished silence. So *that* was the reason for the good behaviour of the twins for the last week.

"And what have you two been up to, to affect your consciences so severely?" Mr. Carstairs demanded sternly.

Jane and Gillian reddened and gulped.

Alison came to their rescue. "It's just a school affair, Daddy," she answered casually. She, too, was intrigued. What *had* Helen done to the twins to make such a lasting impression, she thought amusedly. Usually they bobbed up again unperturbed after a couple of days' disgrace.

"If your consciences are troubling you, it's your own fault," said Mrs. Carstairs, addressing the twins. "And I shall certainly not let it stop Alison from bringing a friend to tea."

"Couldn't we have our tea out—a picnic or something?" Jane ventured desperately. "You'd all enjoy yourselves much better without us," she suggested ingratiatingly.

"Nonsense! A picnic in January! I never heard of such a thing," Mrs. Carstairs said severely.

"We could have it in the woodshed with the animals. It's not cold there," Jane suggested as a last desperate hope.

Her father put his table napkin down decidedly. "You'll either come in here to tea to-morrow and behave politely to Alison's guest, or else you'll go to bed and stay there until she's gone," he stated firmly. "And *without* tea," he added as an afterthought, knowing the twins.

When Helen arrived the next day she found the twins already seated demurely at the tea table. Their cheeks shone with soap, and their hair was damped and sleekly parted in the middle. The faces of the two were expressionless.

Helen smiled upon them in comradely manner as though it was an everyday sight to see such an immaculate pair. As the meal continued, the conversation ranged over various topics, relieved at intervals with friendly laughter. The silent twins began to relax. Apparently Helen had left all school affairs behind her. In fact she seemed to go out of her way to be pleasant to the twins. If they could only last through the meal without embarrassing subjects being brought up, the two juniors felt that they could make their excuses and escape to the safety of the woodshed.

And this they did. They sat on two boxes for a few moments to breathe their relief.

"Gosh! Thank goodness that's over," said Jane. "I thought I should *burst* with goodness."

"With *cream cakes*, you mean," Gillian returned accusingly. "You had *six*."

"No! Did I?" Jane said, licking her lips. "It's surprising how one loses count of that sort of thing. I've been think-ing——" she began in an attempt to change the subject. "About us two. If we've to do things for the school in a year or two, we should start to get ready for it. As I'm no good at lessons I ought to practise at gym and games more. P'raps I might one day even be games captain," she said, letting her imagination run riot.

Gillian sighed. "But *I* shan't," she said sadly. "I *still* can't do that gym exercise properly, even after all the money we've spent on oil. Miss Preston seems to think I'm hopeless."

Jane looked critically at her twin. "I don't somehow think all that money's been wasted," she said. "I heard Mummy tell Daddy that she was surprised how much stronger and fatter you're getting. Nobody can call you skinny now. I expect it's all that oiling and running about I've made you do. I think p'raps you could even do that exercise now if you tried," she suggested. "If you did it once, you'd be awfully bucked. Have a try, it's chilly sitting still."

With Jane's assistance Gillian tried earnestly time after time. They were too engrossed in their efforts to notice the door opening, and two figures standing silently watching.

"It's no use, I just *can't*," Gillian wailed in despair at last. "I'm no better at it than I was. And I *won't* have any more oil rubbed on me. We must have used *gallons* of the beastly, smelling stuff!"

"You don't smell as much as you used to with the other oil

we had," Jane said kindly. "And we've still got a drop left, we mustn't waste it. We can't buy any more until we've paid for those plimsolls, anyway. Come on, have just one more try."

Her twin tried again without success.

"You're not starting off right," Helen's friendly voice broke in as Gillian stood breathlessly on her feet again.

The startled juniors turned towards the doorway.

"Your left foot should be more in front to start with," Helen said, coming forward and deliberately ignoring the sudden strain in the atmosphere. "There, place your foot like this, and now try. I'll help you."

Startled into obedience Gillian did as she was told, and a few moments afterwards she stood triumphantly up again, a dazed smile on her face.

"You've *done* it," Jane breathed, grinning broadly.

"Yes! Now try it again by yourself," Helen suggested encouragingly to Gillian. "*Good*," she exclaimed when she succeeded. "Now you'll always be able to do it."

"Thanks *awfully*," Gillian said shyly.

Jane beamed, forgetting all her embarrassment in the pleasure of her twin's success. "She's been trying for months and *months*," she revealed with satisfaction. "And we must have used *quarts* of oil. I *knew* it wouldn't all be wasted."

"Oil?" Alison asked curiously. "What for?"

Jane opened her eyes wide. "For rubbing on her, of course," she said. "Daddy said it was good for stiff joints, and he's right. He gave us this to try," she disclosed, conscious of the interest of her listeners, and she took down a nauseous-looking bottle from the shelf. "He said this was the best, but we had to change to something else because Gill smelt too much. She was fed up with bathing. It's cost an awful lot of money," Jane finished with a sigh.

There was an extraordinary sound from Alison as she turned hurriedly away. "I—I—please excuse me, I'll be back in a moment," she brought out in strangled tones, and fumbling blindly for the door, she vanished hastily from the shed.

Jane stared after her in anxious surprise. "Isn't she very well, do you think?" she inquired innocently.

Helen bit her lip. " I think she'll be all right in a moment or two," she assured her rather shakily. She pulled herself together. " I'm sorry I gate-crashed into your private sanctum," she said apologetically, thinking it wise to change the subject. " But Alison thought I'd be interested to see your animals," she suggested, looking around.

" Do you *like* animals?" Jane asked.

" Very much," the visitor answered.

Jane's heart warmed towards her. " Then we'll show them to you," she said. " We don't to everybody."

" This is Joey, our parrot," she proclaimed with the air of a showman as she removed the cloth over the cage. We have to keep him covered while Gill does her exercises 'cause he makes rude remarks about it, and it puts her off."

" Good afternoon," said the bird in sepulchral tones, noticing the presence of a stranger.

Jane beamed. " He must like you," she said with relief. " He's not always very polite with visitors." She hastily covered up her pet again before he had time to spoil his reputation, and proceeded to the next exhibit. " And these are our rabbits, Silver and Browny," she said proudly. " They're really Gill's, but we always share everything."

Helen was carefully introduced to each of the pets, in all of which she took suitable interest. She lingered by the cage of white mice, noticing the arrangements made for them.

" Don't you *mind* mice?" Jane inquired.

" Not at all," Helen said with a smile. " We have some at home. My young brother has quite a menagerie of his own."

The twins' eyes widened with interest. " Would you like to *hold* one?" Jane asked, and Helen realised that this was a special honour.

She took the small creature, which ran up her arm and round her neck inquisitively.

The twins were impressed. " They know you like them," Jane exclaimed with pleasure. Her face clouded a little. " Most people don't," she added. " That's why we're afraid they'll gnaw their way out of the cage again, and something'll happen to them."

" Try giving them some food they have to chew hard instead," Helen suggested. " Hard biscuits, and crusts, and so on. They like something to sharpen their teeth on. Then perhaps they'll leave the cage alone."

The twins' voices deepened with respect. " Thank you," they said fervently. " You see, that's why we couldn't keep the puppy," Jane explained, now completely free from embarrassment, " 'cause of them getting out and frightening Mrs. Tompkins."

" Ah," Helen said. " I want to speak to you about that puppy. Shirley can't keep him in her flat. Perhaps you'll let me buy him from you to send to my brother for a birthday present. He's twelve next week."

" We'll *give* him to you, won't we, Gill?" Jane said delightedly. They had been worried about the fate of the puppy, but had felt that it was too delicate a matter to bring up.

" No, I must pay you a proper price for him," Helen replied as a more composed-looking Alison appeared. " It'll help with expenses," she added with a twinkle. " Though I shouldn't spend any more on oil for Gillian, if I were you," she finished, carefully avoiding Alison's eyes. " I think she's outgrown it."

Up in Alison's study-bedroom a quarter of an hour later, Helen and Alison wiped the tears of mirth from their eyes. " *Machine* oil—I ask you! Alison exclaimed in wobbly tones. " And I expect poor Daddy thought they wanted it for creaking door hinges, or something. I—I'm sorry if I appeared rude, dashing away like that," she apologised. " But it was a bit too much for me. I couldn't hurt their feelings. I expect this solves the long-standing mystery of their disappearing pocket money, too," she added with sudden enlightenment.

" They're jolly kids," Helen said. " Nice, too. There's no silly grown-up nonsense about them."

" They're not too bad, really," Alison agreed modestly. " They usually *mean* well, anyway."

CHAPTER FOURTEEN

THE SCHOLARSHIP GIRL

THE NEXT few weeks passed smoothly. There was a different atmosphere in Chester House after Mavis had gone. Good points increased, and order marks and reports lessened.

Brenda was the biggest fly in the ointment. In spite of Helen's hints to her, and the improvement in the standards of Chester House, it seemed as though she could not rid herself of her prejudice against the day girls. Her continual complaints incensed the seniors of the House, and encouraged the juniors to fresh bouts of mischief. Alison tried her best to avoid open conflict with the head of Merton House, but she had a nasty feeling that the bitterness between the two Houses would come to a head one day.

Millchester College had a few openings for scholarship girls. The fees were high, and these free places were keenly sought.

Audrey Weston had won a free place some years before. She was now in the Upper Sixth, where she was studying seriously in the hope of gaining a further scholarship to college. She was a quiet, retiring girl, who did not mix freely with the rest of her form.

Audrey had lost her father in an air disaster two years before and an elder brother was now the main supporter of the family. Audrey had a young sister and their mother was an invalid. Their home was a good distance from the school, and Audrey travelled there on a bicycle, which, to say the least of it, had seen better days. Audrey was sensitive about her bicycle, but she could see no hope of getting a better one, for she knew that her brother was already carrying a financial burden which was too heavy for him.

It was unfortunate that on her arrival at school one morning she met Brenda just leaving the bicycle shed as she was entering it. Brenda was not in the best of moods that morning, matters in her House were troubling her. Mavis was causing difficulties in her House as she had done in Chester House. But this did not make Brenda more sympathetic with the past troubles of the day girls. It merely increased her resentment against them.

It was an unfortunate moment for the two seniors to meet. As Audrey entered the shed she accidentally knocked the prefect's arm with her bicycle, sending the books which Brenda was carrying flying in all directions.

" I'm awfully sorry," Audrey apologised contritely as she propped up her machine and moved forward to help pick up the books. Actually it had not been her fault. Brenda had been too deep in thought to notice her arrival.

" Sorry!" the head of Merton snapped, the last shreds of her frail patience giving way as she ducked to retrieve her belongings. " You day girls go barging about with your bicycles all over the place," she grumbled. Her attention fell on Audrey's bicycle as she straightened herself. " That is, if you *call* it a bicycle," she added bitingly. " How you have the cheek to cycle through the streets on a rusty, broken-down contraption like that, letting the school down, beats me," she said. " I should be ashamed to be seen with it."

Shirley came up to them just in time to hear Brenda's speech, and to notice the white, stricken expression on Audrey's face. She stared with annoyance after the retreating Brenda, and then turned to make some comforting remark to Audrey. But apparently Audrey did not wish for it. She brushed past Shirley with a muttered apology, and hurried away in the direction of the school.

The next day Audrey arrived late. Apparently she had walked, for there was no sign of her bicycle. Alison turned a blind eye on her tardy arrival, knowing that Audrey was a conscientious person who would not be late without a good reason. She knew nothing of the incident with Brenda.

The next morning, prayers were over before Audrey arrived breathlessly. As there was a strict rule on the matter, Alison could not overlook it again.

"She was so odd about it," she confided to Shirley. "She didn't offer any excuse. It's so unlike her."

Shirley moved uncomfortably.

"Helen will want to know the reason for it if she's late again," Alison remarked worriedly.

Shirley cleared her throat. "I doubt if she'll get it," she muttered.

Alison looked sharply at her. "You know something about it, then?" she asked.

Shirley nodded. "I suppose so," she answered unhappily. "I didn't intend to tell anyone, but if Helen's likely to step in you'd better know, privately, anyway."

She told what she had overheard. "Knowing what Brenda is, I hoped Audrey would try to forget it. But it seems to have gone deep. I know the family, they're jolly decent people," Shirley went on. "Since their father died, I suspect that they're pretty hard up. I doubt whether Audrey can *afford* to do anything about the bicycle."

Alison rose to her feet, the light of battle in her eyes. Shirley barred the way as she made for the door. "Where are you off to?" she demanded suspiciously.

"To tell Brenda exactly what I think of her," Alison returned fiercely.

"You're *not*," Shirley answered, standing her ground. "You'll only hurt Audrey more if you have a row about it, and publish her financial difficulties around the school. What I told you was in confidence."

Alison swallowed as she stopped in her tracks. "I suppose you're right, but I feel tearing mad," she confessed, sinking back into her chair, and biting her lip. "Brenda's gone too far this time. But I suppose, as you say, we must guard against Audrey being hurt. I don't want her to get up against Helen, though. Do you think there's hope of her being in time to-morrow?"

"I don't know," Shirley replied. "She's awfully sensitive about it. She feels Brenda's remarks are a reflection on her family. She's walking most of the way at present, she says she

D

feels she can't bring her bicycle to school again. She can't start earlier as she has to wait until someone comes to look after her mother."

" Then I suppose we must leave it at that for the present," Alison said reluctantly.

It did not work out quite that way. Though Alison had decided to drop the matter for a time she could not get it out of her mind. Her anger against Brenda increased as the day wore on. In the afternoon, she returned to the school still fuming. When she entered the cloak-room Brenda was already there, and also in no enviable state of mind. The scene was well set for a clash, though Alison did her best to avoid it. She passed silently through the groups of girls, and, ignoring the head of Merton House, made straight for her locker.

But Brenda was not in the mood to be ignored. She walked over to Alison. " I've been waiting for you," she said. " I've a complaint to make."

Alison sighed. " What, another one !" she answered drily as she hung up her hat. " You seem to be continually making complaints."

Brenda reddened angrily. Conversation in the room had ceased. All present were listening. It was an unheard of thing for two prefects to come to grips in public, let alone the heads of Houses. Alison was aware of that, and she tried to take a hold on herself.

" I don't think this is the time or place for complaints," she said.

" It never *is* the right time for complaints against your House," Brenda answered pointedly.

Alison bit her lip, and glanced at her watch.

" I should be on duty," she said with an effort to control herself. " Can't your complaint, whatever it is, wait until we can discuss it in the prefects' room after school?"

" It will not," Brenda answered bluntly. " That's why I've been trying to speak to you all the morning, to try to avoid more of the hooliganism some members of your House are displaying in the streets. If it's not dealt with before they go home there'll probably be more of it. You must speak to them about it."

Alison's face stiffened. "I don't take orders about my House from anyone but Miss Frazer and Helen," she answered. "If you're referring to three of my juniors who forgot the rules and raced one another to school this morning, I have already dealt with it." It was obvious that Brenda did mean that. "But not under the heading of *hooliganism*," Alison added pointedly. "I don't call it that."

"No, that's the trouble," Brenda muttered meaningly. "The discipline in your House is far too slack. I shouldn't allow my juniors to run wild in the streets like that, but you apparently think lightly of it. I've had to pull up your twin sisters about it more than once."

"I don't make light of it," Alison returned heatedly. "I can deal quite well with such matters without using the bullying, unsympathetic methods you do."

Brenda stared at her. "*Bullying!*" she queried in strangled tones.

"Yes—*bullying*," Alison retorted, forgetting herself entirely, and ignoring Shirley's restraining hand on her arm. "You bully your own House into subjection, but I won't have you bullying mine—juniors *or* seniors," she added with Audrey's hurt in mind.

There was a horrified silence. Brenda's healthy colour faded. She looked shocked.

"I must ask you to withdraw those remarks—the accusations of bullying, anyway," she said in quiet tones for her.

"I shall not do that," Alison returned stubbornly, and her face, too, was pale as she picked up her books and prepared to move off to her delayed duties. "I feel justified in making them. In my opinion the methods you use at times can be described as nothing else *but* bullying," she finished furiously as she swung open the door.

She left consternation behind her.

CHAPTER FIFTEEN

STRIFE BETWEEN THE HOUSES

IT WAS NOT long before wild versions of the scene were circulating around the school. Not by Brenda. To give her her due she kept very quiet on the subject. Her manner afterwards was reserved, and, for her, rather subdued. Only to Helen did she open out when the head girl made inquiries about the quarrel.

"To say that I was a *bully*," Brenda finished when giving an account of the matter. "I hadn't thought that I could be called *that*. I know I'm tactless, you've told me about it plenty of times, but I don't mean to bully anyone."

"Alison said it in the heat of the moment," Helen suggested. "It's easy for the wrong word to slip out when one is angry."

"She meant it, she repeated it several times," Brenda insisted. "I knew she wasn't keen on me, but I didn't think she disliked me as much as that."

"You haven't given her or her House reason to like you, have you?" Helen remarked frankly. "They don't know you as well as I do, and so don't realise that you mean only about half of what you say. They think you've a fixed prejudice against their House, and I must honestly say that I think that's true."

Brenda reddened guiltily.

"Can't you and Alison try to patch things up?" Helen suggested hopefully. "I've already had a word with Alison this morning," she revealed. "I'll admit that I got nowhere with her. There seems to be something behind it all. It's so unlike her," Helen observed worriedly. "There's nothing else she can have against you, is there?"

"I don't think so," Brenda answered doubtfully. "Nothing but the usual rubs as far as I can recollect," she said.

Helen sighed. "Then I wish you'd both clear it up," she said.

" It's common gossip all over the school. If it goes on much longer, there'll be trouble."

" Well," Brenda answered uncertainly, " I shall be surprised if Alison wants any dealings with me, but I'll have a shot at it if you say so, skipper."

Brenda chose an unfortunate moment for her effort. Alison had just seen Audrey emerge unhappily from the head girl's study. Audrey had been later than ever that day, and for this to happen for several days running, in Helen's opinion, needed inquiries made. As Audrey offered no excuse for it, both she and Helen had a bad time. After seeing Audrey's distress, to turn and find the author of it approaching her with intent to speak, was too much for Alison. Being unaware of Brenda's real intention, and fearing that if they met again at that moment it might lead to further trouble, Alison muttered some excuse, and turned away abruptly just as Brenda reached her. She could not trust herself.

Brenda's face darkened as she stared after her. " If *that's* how she feels I'd better leave her to it," she decided bitterly.

By the next day affairs had worsened considerably. A deadly feud appeared to have broken out between the Middles and Juniors of both Houses. Whatever her methods were, Brenda had the support of her House, though it was doubtful if this was brought about by loyalty, or from a sheer love of battle.

Two days passed in this manner with Audrey as late as ever, and the juniors of the two Houses growing more and more unruly.

The usually even-tempered head girl of the school began to lose patience. In trying interviews with both Audrey and Alison, Audrey still refused to give a reason for being later than ever that morning, and Alison stubbornly declined to withdraw her accusations against the head of Merton. The school was in a ferment. Penalties were scattered right and left, but that did not dampen the loyal enthusiasm of the younger girls.

" I could shake the lot of them—Brenda and Alison included," the distracted head girl confided to Jean. " What on earth am I to do with them? Brenda absolutely *asks* for upsets of this kind, and Alison is as stubborn as a mule."

" She always was once she got an idea into her head," Jean replied. " It's that which has given her the grit to dig the day girls out of their rut."

" Yes, and now she's undoing all the good that she's done," Helen said vexedly. " I shall have to put my foot down, but I don't know how. They all seem to have lost their heads, Audrey included, and I could have vouched for her being a sane, level-headed person."

" Ah, Audrey—now that *is* rather odd," Jean agreed. " What are you doing about it?"

" I told her I must report it to the Head if she continues to be late without giving a reason for it," Helen answered.

" Bit strong, isn't it?" Jean objected.

" On the contrary I think it's the kindest thing to do," Helen replied. " It's obvious that Audrey's worried about something which she doesn't feel able to tell me. It might be some home worry she'd find it easier to talk about to Miss Frazer."

" Maybe you're right," Jean agreed. " The Head's an understanding person."

" The difficulty is knowing what is the best thing to do," Helen continued worriedly. " One can't *force* Alison to withdraw her accusation of bullying against Brenda, and that seems to be what the younger girls are squabbling about. The whole school's in a turmoil."

" Maybe things will be easier by to-morrow," Jean tried to comfort her.

Jean's hopes were misplaced. The next day the battle between Chester and Merton Houses was at its height. The mischievous Middles and Juniors of both Houses had spent the previous evening making fresh plans for their attack, glorying in the excuse to pay off a few scores against their long-standing enemies.

Confusion reigned. Audrey arrived at the school in breathless haste long after prayers. Helen's face grew grimmer as the morning went by. Audrey had an interview with her after morning school which left the defaulter more shaken than ever. With sinking heart, Shirley watched Alison that afternoon as she, too, entered the head girl's study. Her friend's expression as she

closed the door behind her rivalled Helen's in its grimness.
Shirley could see that there would be trouble between them.

There was.

As usual Shirley waited for her friend after school. They
cycled home in complete silence. Alison's eyes had a strained
look in them which made Shirley chary about making inquiries.
They slowed down when they reached the side gate of Alison's
home. She dismounted, and would have disappeared with a
hurried farewell if Shirley had not moved swiftly to stop her.

" Come, old thing," she appealed, " we're pals. If something's wrong can't I help?"

Alison looked at her. There was a pinched look about her
mouth. " I don't think you can," she answered evasively. " It's
between Helen and me. We—we've had a row."

" A—a row," Shirley ventured, staring at her. " B—but nobody rows with Helen."

" They do, *I* have," Alison answered stiffly. " Helen's sending Audrey to Miss Frazer if she's late again to-morrow, and it
was the last straw."

" Oh," Shirley said. " But I suppose Helen had to do something about it. It's her job," she added fairly.

" While the real author of the trouble gets off scot free?"
Alison returned bitterly.

" Can't you tell Helen about Audrey?" Shirley ventured.
" She'd understand."

" No," Alison answered emphatically. " There's enough gossip
going round the school without dragging Audrey's private affairs
into it. I told her I'd try to avoid that, and I can't break my
word just to spare myself," she finished in odd tones.

" You—you mean——?" Shirley queried unsteadily.

" I mean," Alison answered bluntly, " that there's to be a
special school council meeting about it, and Helen has asked me
not to attend."

Shirley gazed at her. " B—but I don't understand," she said
shakily.

" I do," Alison answered in bleak tones. " It means that
Helen blames me for the upset in the school. I may be responsible for some of it," she owned. " I shouldn't have made my

accusations against Brenda in public. Helen thinks that I'm refusing to withdraw them as a matter of pride, but it's not all that. I feel there was reason for it when I see what's happening to Audrey. I lost my temper and Helen got worked up. She said that if I don't try to put things right with Brenda by to-morrow, I'm suspended from the council."

Shirley swallowed hard. " B—but you can't possibly let that happen," she exclaimed.

" I can," Alison answered stubbornly. " I bear Helen no ill will over it," she added ruefully. " She had to do something."

" But you can't let her suspend you," Shirley protested agitatedly. " It might lead to——" She faltered.

" My losing my prefectship and house headship, too, I suppose you mean," Alison finished flatly for her. " In that case you must carry on for me."

" I can't and I *won't*," Shirley answered fiercely. " It's a lot of nonsense. If you're not free to tell Helen about Audrey, *I* am. That's at the bottom of the trouble. Helen will see your point when she knows that."

" You'll do nothing of the kind," Alison answered heatedly. " I won't have Audrey dragged into it."

" But she *is* in it," Shirley protested urgently. " She wouldn't want you to lose your prefectship just to protect her feelings."

" That's for me to decide," Alison replied. " I'm still head of the House."

" You may be," Shirley conceded unhappily. " But you're not acting like it, or you'd put the good of the House before your own feelings and Audrey's. Helen's a decent person, she wouldn't let Audrey be hurt, you know that." She gulped. " I—I think Helen's right," she continued shakily. " It *is* a matter of stubborness and pride with you as well as with Audrey, though there's excuse for Audrey as she is the one who was hurt."

They argued for some time, growing more and more heated over it, until at last, feeling thoroughly miserable, Shirley made her way home. It was the first time that the two friends had quarrelled. They both spent a sleepless night.

CHAPTER SIXTEEN

HELEN TAKES A STAND

SHIRLEY was up early the next day. After hours of quiet thought she had come to a decision. If Alison was not willing to do anything to help herself then someone who cared for her must make the attempt instead.

Shirley swallowed a quick breakfast and hurried to school. Helen was in the habit of arriving there extra early, she knew.

The head girl looked up with a slight smile as Shirley entered her study. It was clear that Helen, too, had had a troubled night. She looked pale and worried.

"Hallo, you're early," she said, glancing at her watch.

"I—I want a private talk with you," Shirley explained nervously.

"What's the trouble?" Helen asked encouragingly, when she had settled her plainly agitated visitor in a comfortable chair.

Haltingly Shirley told her the full story. Conflicting emotions crossed Helen's face as she listened. Occasionally she inserted a query to make some point clear, but that was all. She sat in silence for a few moments when Shirley finished.

"I'm grateful to you for coming and explaining things," she said. "It'll be a great help. You know," she added thoughtfully, "I don't expect Brenda has the faintest idea that she has upset Audrey. She's like that. She has about as much tact as a charging hippopotamus, but she's not really hard. She doesn't realise the financial difficulties some people have to cope with. It's time that she did." She paused. "We'd better keep this talk private for the moment," she murmured. "I must think out what is best to do."

"I shall be glad to," Shirley agreed soberly. "Alison'll be furious when she knows that I've been to you."

"She needn't know, as far as I'm concerned," Helen said. "I

admire Alison," she observed. " She's done a grand bit of work on your House, but she hasn't been as helpful over this business as she might have been. She was very difficult yesterday afternoon, and I couldn't see the point of it. I understand now that she was worried about Audrey."

The day wore on, with the Middles and Juniors of both Houses still thoroughly enjoying the heat of battle, and the wearied prefects growing more exasperated every moment.

Alison and Audrey went though the day expecting calamity to fall on them at any moment. When school finished in the afternoon they both departed homewards in a slightly bewildered state.

After school Brenda went along quite unsuspectingly to the head girl's study when she heard that she wished to see her.

" It's about this trouble between your House and Chester," Helen began. " Something will have to be done about it."

" Well, I'm not encouraging the kids to scrap with each other," Brenda retorted rather crossly.

" No," Helen said, " and neither is Alison. The only way to stop it is to get down to the cause of it."

" The cause?" Brenda returned. " I suppose you mean the row between Alison and me?" she suggested.

" Yes," Helen answered evenly. " The youngsters are quarrelling over their separate loyalties to you and Alison. Take away your differences and you take away theirs."

" Maybe," Brenda blustered, " but if you're working yourself up to ask me to apologise to Alison again you're wasting your breath. I'm not going to be insulted again as I was before."

" No, I don't think unwilling apologies of that sort are likely to do much good," Helen said. " It'd be like grafting new skin on a festering sore. It would only break through again."

Brenda stared at her. " What are you talking about?" she said. Imagination was not her strongest point, which was probably the reason why she so often blundered.

" I mean," Helen told her carefully, " that the trouble between your Houses has reached the stage where it needs more than a half-hearted apology to cure it. I blame myself for some of it. I said at the beginning of the school year that I intended to suppress the ill feelings between the Houses. By that I mean the attitude of superiority which some boarders adopt towards the day girls. You've been the chief offender there, I'm afraid."

Brenda looked taken aback.

Helen spoke more plainly. "Hasn't it occurred to you, as I suggested before, that Alison may feel she has a genuine complaint against you?" she said carefully.

Brenda jumped to her feet, her eyes blazing. "Are you trying to tell me that you believe Alison's accusations against me of bullying?" she almost bellowed.

"*Sit down and stop shouting,*" Helen said firmly. "There are still people in the school, remember!"

Brenda obeyed. She gulped frantically, but still glared angrily at her form-mate.

"I shouldn't call you a bully," Helen went on in quiet tones. "But then I know you better than most people. We've been here at Millchester together ever since we were ten years old." And Helen smiled a little at the thought of those past mischievous days. "We've lived, and worked, and played together most of that time, and—and, well I've grown fond of you," she confessed. "I hate to see you setting everyone by the ears, and covering up what a decent soul you really are. As I've told you before you don't realise what hurt you can do with that sharp tongue of yours."

Brenda gulped. Helen's affectionate speech had moved her. "Well, what have I done now?" she asked in suppressed tones.

"It's Audrey Weston," Helen told her. "Haven't you noticed that she's been late in the morning for the last week?"

"I have," Brenda answered. "But it's nothing to do with me."

"But it *is*, and it's plain that most of the trouble arises from it," Helen replied.

Brenda stared at her blankly. "I don't know what you mean," she said.

Helen told her. From Brenda's expression as she listened it was clear that she had quite forgotten the incident with Audrey until she was reminded of it.

"I may have said something of the sort," she admitted

vaguely. "But there's no crime in that, surely. Anybody should be ashamed to bring a filthy machine like that to the school."

"It was not filthy," Helen said. "I noticed that. It was merely rusty from age and use. There was no need to hurt Audrey's feelings like that."

"But surely she could do something about it," Brenda protested. "She could get another bicycle, have it overhauled, or— or something."

"Which would cost money," Helen pointed out quietly.

"Eh?" Brenda looked dense.

Helen stifled a sigh. "The trouble is that you've always had an easy time as far as money is concerned," she remarked. "You don't realise the difficulties some people are up against. I've noticed that Audrey doesn't join clubs, and so on, and I suspect that it's because she can't afford the subscriptions. But the bicycle is a necessity. She can't get to school in time without it. She has her family to see to, and an invalid mother to make comfortable before she starts for school. She can't come until someone relieves her."

Brenda was still staring: Such revelations were quite new to her.

"But why does Audrey come to a school like this if she can't live up to its standards?" she said. "There must be more suitable places for people like that."

Then the sorely tried head girl suddenly lost both her dignity and her patience. "Really, Brenda, you're the absolute *end!*" she exclaimed vexedly. "That snobbish nonsense went out ages ago. Decent people don't judge others by the amount of money they have, but by what they *do*. Millchester *needs* people like Audrey. She may appear rather insignificant and retiring, but if she hadn't turned it down because of her home ties she might have been a school prefect and head of her House by now. As it is, with her brains she's likely to win high honours for the school, which will last when people like you and I, who imagine that we're important, are quite forgotten. You make me ashamed to hear you talk so."

"So I'm a snob as well as a bully, am I?" Brenda brought

out in strangled tones. She was pale, and both of them were very near tears.

Helen rose to her feet. "Not really, as I know you," she answered quietly, "but I'll leave you to think it out for yourself. You love Millchester as much as I do," she went on in unsteady tones, "and it's clear that the key to the solution of its present problems is in your hands." She moved towards the door, not trusting herself to look again at the stricken, despondent figure of her friend as she sat slumped in her chair. She must not let herself weaken.

Alone in the study, the head of Merton bowed her head over the table, at first in stricken silence, but then the tears came. Helen's words had gone right home.

CHAPTER SEVENTEEN

A VISIT FROM BRENDA

BRENDA'S MIND was a jumble of emotions as she pedalled along through the busy streets in the gathering dusk. She might be going on a fruitless errand, she knew, yet she could not rest that night until she had made some move. In all their years together she had not seen Helen as angry as she had been that afternoon, and for it to have to be with her! Brenda swallowed painfully as she swerved to avoid a car. In doing so, her eyes were attracted by a patch of colour in a window which she was passing. She cycled by, slowed down, and then turned back. After another short examination of the window, she propped up her bicycle and went into the shop. A few minutes afterwards she emerged, and, tucking her purchase into her bicycle basket, she pedalled away.

She halted at a small house in a quiet street, and paused nervously before ringing the bell.

A bright-looking girl of about twelve years of age opened the door. She looked curiously at the senior. "Does Audrey Weston live here?" Brenda inquired, and the girl nodded.

"Yes," she answered politely.

"Then may I speak to her for a moment?" the senior asked. The child smiled. "I'll tell her," she said.

A few moments afterwards, Audrey appeared at the door. She could not quite hide her shocked dismay when she saw the visitor. Brenda noticed it.

"I know I'm not welcome," she said in low tones. "But could I have a private talk with you? I needn't keep you many minutes."

Audrey asked her in. Brenda paused to pick up the parcel she had placed in her basket, and followed her into a quiet, pleasantly furnished room. Audrey closed the door carefully behind them. She offered her visitor a chair, but she did not accept it.

"No, I'll get what I have to say off my chest first," she said in subdued tones. "I owe you an apology. I—I didn't realise that I had upset you until this afternoon when Helen told me about it. It's about your bicycle."

Audrey's mouth quivered a little. "Yes," she said.

"I—I'm sorry I made the remarks I did," Brenda went on. "I'm afraid I'm very dense about some things. Apart from anything else, I was very rude, I can see that."

There was an odd look on Audrey's face. "I didn't know that Helen knew about it," she said. "Did she tell you to come?"

"No, *nobody* knows that I have come," Brenda said. "But I felt that I had to do something before the morning in case you were late again."

Audrey stood silent for a while. "Helen's vexed, but I can't help being late," she said simply. "I can't leave Mother until our help comes."

"Helen was more worried than vexed," Brenda told her. "It appears that you didn't tell her why you couldn't be on time." She paused. "The skipper's furious with me," she then said, and Audrey was amazed to see the lips of the reputedly hard-hearted head of Merton quivering suspiciously. "She thinks that my upsetting you is the real cause of the present trouble in the school."

Audrey's eyes widened in dismay. "But surely everyone doesn't know about m—my bicycle?" she said, colouring sensitively.

"Not at all," Brenda assured her hastily. "Only two or three of us. The kids are squabbling about the upset between Alison and myself. Helen thinks that wouldn't have happened if Alison hadn't been upset about you."

"Oh," said Audrey in thoughtful surprise.

There was another short silence. "I—I know it's cheek of me after what's happened," Brenda ventured uncertainly. "But I—I wonder whether you'll try to forget things and consider cycling to school as usual to-morrow so that we can start to put things right. I shall never get straight with Alison until you do. It's for the school, and not for myself, I'm asking," she added.

There was a long pause. Audrey looked straight at the prefect. "It's not easy," she said in low, embarrassed tones. "But I'll try my best. Perhaps my brother can patch up my bicycle a bit. Anyway, I'll do what I can," she promised.

"Thanks, that's decent of you," Brenda said, swallowing a lump in her throat. She was feeling more and more ashamed of herself as she realised her form-mate's difficulties. She turned hastily aside, and picked up the parcel she had brought. She thrust it self-consciously towards Audrey. "I—I saw these in a shop window, and thought your mother might like them," she said awkwardly as she started to go.

Audrey stopped her. "Thank you very much," she said earnestly, and with softened expression she sniffed at the early spring flowers. "Mother loves flowers. I—I suppose," she suggested tentatively, "you wouldn't like to see her and give her them yourself? She likes visitors, and this is one of her best days."

Brenda was not used to illness, but she took this offer as an honour, as indeed it was. "Thanks, I should like to," she said.

"You won't mention why you came, or let her suspect anything will you?" Audrey queried anxiously before she opened the door.

She led her visitor into another pleasant room which had a comfortable, lived-in appearance about it. On a couch by the window lay a frail, sweet-faced little lady. Her tired eyes lit up with pleasure at the sight of a visitor.

"This is Brenda, one of the seniors from the school, Mother," Audrey said. "She's brought you some flowers."

"And this is my sister, Anne," she added, indicating the girl who had opened the door, who now rose from her place at the side of her mother, and politely offered her chair to the visitor.

Brenda accepted it rather awkwardly, wondering what to say to the invalid. She need not have worried.

"My dear," said Mrs. Weston, as she sniffed at the sweet-smelling violets and primroses, "you couldn't have brought me anything to give me greater pleasure. It's my first touch of spring."

Brenda smiled, feeling well repaid for her thought.

"I'm pleased, too, to meet one of Audrey's form-mates," the invalid went on in her gentle voice. "I wish she'd bring more of them here," she added with a loving look at Audrey, who had returned to the room with a bowl of water for the flowers. "She doesn't have as much social life as she should."

Audrey smiled back at her. It was plain that there was comradeship between the two. "Brenda is a boarder, Mother," she said. "Her home isn't in the town."

"Oh," Mrs. Weston answered with interest. "I know what that means. I was a boarder at school myself for a number of years. It has its benefits as well as its drawbacks, hasn't it?"

Brenda agreed that it had.

"Yes," Mrs. Weston continued with a reminiscent sigh. "We had some fun, and got up to some high old pranks. I suppose it's the same to-day?" she said.

Brenda smiled, but did not commit herself.

"Brenda is a school prefect, and head of Merton House," Audrey explained casually before she disappeared again.

Mrs. Weston's eyes twinkled. "Which remark, I suppose, is meant as a warning not to incriminate you," she said with an infectious little laugh in which Brenda found herself joining.

Conversation went easily after that. The younger girl listened with interest to the talk as her mother gradually drew the senior out until they were laughing and talking freely. Audrey, in the next room, was astonished to hear the much-feared head of Merton in such a mood. Brenda's voice was soft, and her manner gentle with her frail listener.

"You must come again," Mrs. Weston told her. "Perhaps you'll have tea with us one day."

Audrey, who was entering the room on some domestic duty, held her breath. Brenda gave her a quick glance.

"Thank you, I should like to," she answered softly.

"We must find a convenient time for you," Mrs. Weston said. "Can you get out often, or are you near enough to your home to go there in your free time?"

Brenda lowered her head a little. "I have no settled home," she said. "My father is abroad most of the time, and my mother died when I was small. I'm the only child."

Mrs. Weston's motherly face softened in concern. "I'm sorry, perhaps I shouldn't have asked," she said. But from that moment she took the lonely girl to her heart.

"Anne, here, has won a scholarship to your school," she said, thinking it best to change the subject. "She hopes to start in the autumn."

The younger girl smiled shyly at the visitor. "Yes, but only as a day girl," she said. "I couldn't leave Mummy."

She eyed Brenda with respect. She had heard from Audrey what great beings in the school the heads of houses were, and here was one actually in her home. Her awe was not lessened by the number of school tales which she had devoured.

"I couldn't spare her or her sister," Mrs. Weston said affectionately. "I don't know what we should do without Audrey," she added. "She's a great comfort to us all." She broke off as Audrey entered the room again. "Audrey is making tea for her brother," she said. "Will you have a cup, too?"

Brenda glanced at her watch and jumped hastily to her feet. "Thank you very much, but I mustn't," she exclaimed. "It's later than I thought. I said I wouldn't be long, and I've another call to make."

Audrey saw her to the door, her sober face brighter than it had been for days. " Thanks for being so kind to Mother," she said sincerely. " It's done her the world of good. I—I—she would like you to come again, I know."

Brenda stopped on the doorstep to look straight into the eyes of the day girl. "And would *you* like me to come?" she demanded.

Audrey's look did not flinch. "I certainly would," she answered honestly.

"Thanks, then I will," Brenda said. "I'm glad that young sister of yours is coming to Millchester," she went on. " She seems a nice child, the sort we want. I don't know whether you realise it, but you're a jolly lucky person one way and another," she added gruffly to Audrey's surprise, before she mounted her bicycle and pedalled away.

Audrey gazed after her thoughtfully, suddenly seeing her form-mate as she really was, and as Helen knew her. Could it be, Audrey thought pityingly, that the main reason for Brenda's antagonism towards Chester House was not caused by snobbishness, as was supposed, but by her loneliness and an understandable envy of the day girls in their more secure and happy homes.

From that moment the wall of prejudice between Chester and Merton Houses began to totter.

A few more bricks fell when ten minutes afterwards, Brenda presented herself at the home of the Carstairs family.

The door was opened by the mice-ridden Mrs. Tompkins. She left Brenda standing in the hall. Miss Alison was in her room, she said. She would tell her she was wanted.

As the senior waited, a door in the hall burst open and the twins emerged noisily. Catching sight of the visitor, they gasped with dismay and hurriedly retreated back into the room again, closing the door behind them. Brenda could hear the sound of agitated whispering coming from the room. She bit her lip ruefully.

Alison appeared and came down the stairs towards her. She hid her astonishment more carefully than the twins. Her face was expressionless as she neared her form-mate.

"May I speak to you privately for a moment?" Brenda suggested tentatively.

Alison hesitated, and then invited her upstairs to her study-bedroom. There was no privacy downstairs when the twins were about. It was obvious from the books spread on her table that Alison had been busy with her preparation.

"I mustn't stop," Brenda said when the door was closed, and she was offered a chair. "I'm late as it is. I came to tell you that I've been to see Audrey." She paused. "I've apologised to her for what I said the other day, and she has accepted it. She hopes to cycle to school to-morrow." Brenda halted again, and then went on as Alison was still silent. "I only realised to-day that I'd upset her so badly. I'm in a pretty bad row with the skipper about it. She said that there would be no peace between our two Houses until it was put right. She thinks that's why we two quarrelled. Is that right?"

"Mainly, I think," Alison agreed slowly.

"I realise that I haven't been too tactful in other ways, either," Brenda admitted. "And I agree with Helen that in the case of Audrey there was perhaps reason for your remarks." She paused again. "After all, we're two Houses, but only one school," she appealed quietly. "Can't we try to sink our differences for its benefit?"

Alison stood silent for a moment, battling with herself, then suddenly she thrust out her hand. "I haven't been without blame, either," she owned. "If Audrey is happy about things then so am I."

Brenda took the offered hand. "Thanks," she said huskily. "I'll call and tell Helen on my way back."

CHAPTER EIGHTEEN

A FRESH START

BRENDA never went half-way with anything. Audrey was astonished the next morning when she emerged from her home to find the prefect waiting for her.

"Thought I'd just look round and make sure you're able to cycle to school this morning," the head of Merton offered as excuse in matter of fact tones, as though it was a mere nothing for her to have gone a couple of miles out of her way at that busy time of the morning. "I thought if your bicycle wasn't workable you might borrow mine for to-day as it's important for you to be on time."

"Thanks, it's jolly decent of you," Audrey answered. "But my brother has patched up my bicycle for this morning. He's seeing about another one for me by Monday."

She looked doubtfully at her decrepit machine, and then at Brenda. "It looks pretty awful, I know," she said apologetically. "If you'd rather go on alone I shall quite understand."

Brenda coloured, remembering her remarks on that subject. "Don't be ridiculous," she answered irritably. "I don't know what I'm talking about at times."

They were greeted with surprised stares as they wheeled their bicycles through the school grounds. Brenda affected not to notice it. The astonishment of the groups of seniors gathered in the cloakroom was even more marked than that of the younger girls outside. Alison was changing her shoes but at the sudden silence, she looked up to see the reason for it. Her eyes met Brenda's, the rest held their breaths. This had been the previous battle-ground of the two heads of Houses. For a second or two Alison hesitated. Brenda had gone out of her way to do her bit, she decided, it was up to her now. She turned and moved towards the newcomers.

"Good," she said with a smile which embraced both Brenda and Audrey. "I was looking out for you two. I'm glad you managed it, Audrey." She turned to Brenda. "Miss Thompson wants to see me before school," she said. "Will you do me a favour and take over my cloak-room duty for this morning if I do yours to-morrow? I'll make it right with Helen."

Brenda nodded, and they moved away together.

Helen looked a different person when they both came to her room to partake of their milk and biscuits at morning-break.

"Jolly good," she beamed. "Now we can start to tackle your younger fry."

The feud was dead. There was no doubt about that. It gave its last expiring groans during the next few days in spite of the efforts of a number of venturesome juniors to revive it.

Alison took up the reins firmly in her House. She deeply regretted her share in the setback of the last week. No efforts on her part would be spared, she decided, to help wipe out its ill effect. An appalling number of order marks had accumulated in the reports book. They must be balanced somehow if the House was not once more to grace the bottom of the list in the end-of-year results.

She took stock of her assets. In the way of games, they were definitely improving, she knew. Rita was a live wire as captain. Her team had already drawn with one of the other Houses in a friendly game. She meant to go all out for a higher place in the end-of-term hockey matches, Rita informed the head of the House. *And*, she told Shirley fiercely, it was up to her to get practice at her strokes in readiness for the next term's tennis. Shirley meekly agreed, for though she was naturally modest about her prowess with the racquet, she realised that as far as tennis was concerned she was the main hope of her House.

There was still a term and a half before the end of the school year, Alison thought. It would allow time for some of the girls to produce entries for the hobbies and handicraft section of the school's annual exhibition, which took place towards the end of the summer term. Alison impressed these and other matters forcefully on her House. Her appeal produced enthusiasm from

the majority of the girls. Jane, however, thought it necessary to
deride the idea.

"What's the use of asking us to enter stuff from our hobbies
for the exhibition?" she observed gloomily. "*Our* hobbies are
alive. If we enter George and Blossom everybody'll start screaming. And if we took Joey he'd be sure to bring out his worst bad
word in front of Miss Frazer, or else he'd make rude remarks
about her hat. You know what he is."

Gillian giggled.

"S'nothing to laugh at," Jane continued glumly. "I can't
make *anything* with my hands, you know what my sewing and
knitting look like. *You* can sew and paint and make decent
things."

Gillian looked thoughtful. "I don't think you've got it quite
right," she said. "Alison meant that we should try to do *something* for the House, not just with our hands. I can sew and
paint a bit," she admitted modestly. "But you can do things I
can't—like gym, and games, and swimming, and running,
and——"

She stopped abruptly at a sudden shout from her twin.
"*That's* it!" Jane yelled wildly.

"Wh—what is?" Gillian inquired in bewilderment, looking
anxiously around.

"*Swimming*," her twin retorted excitedly. "I'll swim, and
swim, and swim, and——"

"Sounds like a goldfish," Gillian remarked.

Jane ignored it. "I mean I'll swim and swim, and practise
and practise until I get into the House swimming team for the
sports. Perhaps if I do I can get a few points for our House.
I can swim fairly well, can't I?" she ventured, modestly for her.

Gillian's face lit up with affectionate pride in her twin.
"You're a jolly good swimmer," she said fervently. "I'm sure
you can get into the team if you practise a lot. I'll time you at
it."

"Then that's settled," Jane sighed with relief. "I'll swim
and you'll sew and paint, and we'll make the rest of our crowd
do something, too. We've been pretty awful lately, and it'll help
to make up the marks we've lost. It'll be a peaceful way of

tackling those Merton girls if we can beat them at something," she added with a grin. " If Alison says we mustn't *fight* them I'll *swim* them out instead."

Alison saw that the newly roused enthusiasm in her House did not wane. Apart from any hopes she cherished about placing Chester House higher on the end of year's list, she wisely decided that to keep her subjects interested and busy was the best way of keeping them out of mischief.

" It's worse than when she first took over the House," Joyce complained wearily. " Chivvy, chivvy, *chivvy*. She achieves her end as far as I'm concerned, anyway. I'm glad to escape to the music room for extra practice to gain a little peace."

Her fellow seniors laughed. They were all suffering in some way from the inexhaustible driving energy of the head of their House. But it did not lessen her popularity with them. She was responsible for the improved standards of their House, they well knew, and there was now a more friendly feeling between Chester House and the boarders than there had ever been.

CHAPTER NINETEEN

TAKING STOCK AT THE END OF THE YEAR

THE END of the Easter term drew near. Pauline and the other senior chosen travelled to London to sit for the Pendleton Scholarship Examination, the results of which would not be known for some weeks.

The hockey matches between the Houses took place the last week of the term. Rita could be heard haranguing her team at every available opportunity. They were drawn to meet Oakley House for the first match.

There were quite a few girls present from all of the Houses on the afternoon that the match took place, although the result of the match was a foregone conclusion, or so some of them thought. Chester House had always been disgracefully weak at the game.

But those present were more than interested when at half-time the score stood even—two goals to each House.

The second half of the game took place with mounting excitement on the part of the onlookers. Rita's face was stiff with effort and determination, which she had also tried to instil into her team. But time passed and it appeared as though the game must end in a draw. Oakley House team, too, was exerting itself to the utmost. All eyes were on the field when ten minutes before the game was due to finish Rita tore across the field and, with a well-judged shot, sent the ball speeding through the posts.

There was a roar of excitement from most of the onlookers. Oakley House was looking a little shocked. Their team were definitely out for blood during the next ten minutes. Their attitude suggested that they meant to get that extra goal or die in the attempt. But the vital minutes passed. Jane was almost dancing with anxiety. Her voice topped those of the rest of the onlookers.

" Go it, Rita! Up with the Chesters!" she yelled in tones which made those near her clap their hands to their heads.

The whistle went with no further goals scored. The victorious team from Chester House accepted the congratulations of their slightly bewildered opponents and happily made their way back to the school.

" Our first score over one of the Houses for many a long day," Alison remarked with warm satisfaction to the captain of their team. " Jolly good going, Rita."

Rita grinned. " It's gained a few points for us, anyway," she said. " I doubt whether we shall manage as well in the next round. It depends on who we have to face. Anyway, we shan't be at the bottom of the list this time."

It turned out more or less as Rita said. Her team finished with a draw in their next match. At the end of the term, Jean's team from Russell House took their usual place at the head of the hockey list, Chester House coming fourth instead of sixth as they usually were.

"Next year, when we've had more practice and Jean has left, we'll have a shot at taking her place at the head of the list," Rita predicted hopefully.

That summer term was a happy one. From its beginning, with the encouragement of its head, Chester House was a hive of industry.

Jane swam in fine weather or wet with Gillian giving her sisterly encouragement as she timed her from the side. Unsuspected by either of them, some of the seniors were taking interested note of Jane's progress.

To that junior's consternation, one morning just before half-term, she received a summons from Brenda. With much searching of conscience she unwillingly obeyed. She could not think of anything *particularly* bad that she had done recently.

She emerged from the prefects' room to her waiting twin looking more stunned than ever. Her eyes were wide with surprise.

"What *do* you think?" she said in dazed tones. "Y'know Brenda's school swimming captain. She says she's had a challenge from Woodgate School for a junior swimming match, and she says if I keep on improving I might get a chance to be in the team. She's going to coach me herself. *Me* to p'raps swim for the school!" she exclaimed, her voice rising to a squeal with excitement as she fully grasped the fact.

Gillian's face beamed with pride in her twin.

It was a week of happenings. The next day, Pauline received a request to attend for an interview connected with the Pendleton Scholarship. This meant that she was one of the chosen six from whom would be selected the fortunate holder of the scholarship for the next three years.

Pauline departed for London, looking nervous and anxious, but cheered on by the good wishes of her friends.

She was not present when the school assembled for prayers the next morning. Neither was Miss Frazer. Her assistant conducted the short service. But just as it finished, and the girls were about to be dismissed to their form-rooms, the headmistress arrived, and held up her hand for silence.

"Girls," she said, and her voice was full of emotion. "I have just received a 'phone call. The Pendleton Scholarship has been won by a senior of our school—Pauline Cartwright of Chester House!"

Pandemonium was let loose. The girls of every House cheered and cheered. It was the first time the school had won the coveted honour for many years. It basked itself in Pauline's reflected glory.

"Whatever we poor ordinary mortals achieve, it will be just a drop in the ocean after Pauline's scoop," Joyce observed lazily a few days later.

"Nonsense," Alison answered briskly, smiling at the blushing Pauline. "Pauline's done her bit, and now it's up to the rest of us."

Joyce sighed. "I *thought* I might indulge in a few moments' rest before my exam to-morrow," she complained as she dragged herself to her feet and picked up her instrument. "But be it on your own head if I collapse from overwork and nervous strain." And she departed for the music-room.

The rest of the prefects chuckled. The idea of the languid Joyce overworking herself in any way was comical.

The last week of the school year arrived, a time of sadness for some of the seniors. The prefects of Chester House were gathered together for their last official meeting. There was little business, most of the time was spent in taking stock of their past efforts.

"We started off badly," Alison said, "which was partly my fault. But things have improved lately. Goodness knows how our marks compare with other Houses, though. Any ideas on that point, Shirley?" Shirley kept the records of the House.

"Not really," Shirley answered. "One never knows how Miss Frazer will mark things. Order marks have been considerably less lately——"

"Nobody's had any spare time to collect any," Joyce remarked with a teasing look at Alison. They all smiled.

"But on the other hand," Shirley continued, "we must have collected a few extra marks of merit. There's Pauline's effort topping the list, and Joyce's success in her exam." For Joyce had managed a pass, though she had not gained the distinction hoped for. "Then there's Audrey with her scholarship to Chauncy College."

"Yes, I'm glad about that," Alison interposed. "She deserved a break."

There was a murmur of agreement. The result of Audrey's examination had just been received. Chauncy College was on the outskirts of Millchester, and easily reached from Audrey's home, making it possible for her to continue with her duties towards her family.

"In games, too, thanks to Rita, we've done a bit better than last year," Shirley went on, referring to the notes before her. "In hockey we're farther up the list. Tennis and cricket are not quite as good."

"Which in the case of tennis was not your fault," Rita interposed. "You played jolly well. It was bad luck that you were drawn against last year's champion."

"Maybe," Shirley answered mildly. She glanced again at her records, and went on. "We scored a few points in small success in athletics, and in swimming——" She broke off, and her mouth broadened into a grin. "Really, that Jane!" she exclaimed.

They all smiled.

"I believe she'll be a leading light at it one of these days," Rita observed. "Swam like a fish, didn't know she had it in her," she went on. "She grabbed that junior cup for our House almost on her own. Didn't do too badly for the school, either."

"Yes," Jane's elder sister agreed modestly. "But for goodness sake don't tell her so," she added in mock dismay. "I have to live with her, remember, and my prefectly powers of suppression have almost run out."

They laughed again.

"I may be wrong, but in my opinion of the twins," Pauline said thoughtfully, "it is Gillian who'll be making the greatest mark on this House in the future. She's a clever kid."

"Yes, that painting and sewing of hers was very good," Joyce remarked. "Got first prize and gathered a few marks in for us, didn't she?"

"I didn't mean that," Pauline answered. "I've seen some of

her ordinary school work. Her essays in particular look pretty brainy to me."

This from the brilliant Pauline was a compliment indeed.

Shirley's eyes twinkled. "Looks as though the Carstairs family is going to *haunt* this House for a while," she remarked, grinning at her friend.

Her words were echoed to some extent a day or two later when the marks for the Houses were read out to the assembled school.

"The results this year are extraordinary," the headmistress remarked, "in that there is only *one* mark between the two Houses which head the list." The school was stilled with excitement. "I know that there will be disappointment on the part of the losers, but I think you will realise how surprised and gratified I was when I saw who were the holders of the House cup for next year. Chester House heads the list, with Russell House running it close with only one mark less."

For a few moments the school was stunned, winners and losers alike. But then there was a burst of cheering from the rest of the girls, while Chester House looked bashful at the glory so suddenly thrust upon them.

Miss Frazer lifted her hand for silence.

"I cannot let this moment pass without offering special congratulations to the winning House. This first victory of theirs has not been won easily. They have had serious setbacks. It's only through hard work from all of the House that they have won their place at the top of the list." Miss Frazer paused then went on. "I especially commend the prefects of this House for their unswerving support of their leader, Alison Carstairs, whose grit and determination have helped to win for her House the high place it now holds in the school."

Alison was pale with emotion. Helen caught the headmistress's eyes.

"Another three cheers for Chester House and its leader!" she called clearly.

The hall rang.